THE WIDOW
Ilsa Mayr

When Santiago, the tough-looking, scarred, but oddly attractive cowboy carrying a caged, one-winged macaw and a baby, approaches Jane Peterson for a job on her south Texas ranch, warning bells go off. Reasoning that a man tenderly caring for two helpless beings cannot be dangerous, she hires him.

The independent, hardworking widow needs help, as she is beset by dangers: the brutal drought plaguing the land, the illegal border crossings on her ranch, the mysterious happenings on her high mesa. Yet the biggest danger is Santiago. Having sworn on her husband's grave that she would never fall for another man in love with danger, she is still helplessly drawn to Santiago.

Threatened with bank foreclosures and Santiago's deportation by Immigration, Jane and Santiago find an unorthodox solution. Marrying a U.S. citizen allows Santiago to stay in the country, while his savings rescue the ranch. Secretly, both hope that this marriage of convenience will turn into a loving union. Before that can happen, they battle nature as well as greed, hate, and revenge.

AVALON BOOKS

THE WIDOW

•

Ilsa Mayr

AVALON BOOKS
NEW YORK

For Jamie, with thanks

Published by Avalon Books,
an imprint of Thomas Bouregy & Co., Inc.
160 Madison Avenue, New York, NY 10016

Library of Congress Cataloging-in-Publication Data

Mayr, Ilsa.
  The widow / Ilsa Mayr.
      p.   cm.
  ISBN 978-0-8034-7605-9 (hardcover : acid-free
paper) 1. Widows—Fiction. 2. Ranch life—Texas—
Fiction. 3. Mexican-American Border Region—
Fiction. I. Title.
  PS3613.A97W53   2011
  813'.6—dc22   2011018709

PRINTED IN THE UNITED STATES OF AMERICA
ON ACID-FREE PAPER
BY RR DONNELLEY, BLOOMSBURG, PENNSYLVANIA

Prologue

Guatemala

*A*mbush!

Even as the leader of the small group realized that the jungle clearing was unnaturally quiet, it was already too late.

A hail of bullets trapped the group in a deadly cross fire. Santiago squeezed the trigger of the M-16, swinging it in a ninety-degree arc, determined to take as many of the ambushers with him as he could. From the corner of his eye he saw his sister fall, shielding the baby with her body. Before he could call out to Corazon, he felt a bullet rip into his right side and another gouge a searing path along his skull. A red haze obscured his sight, and he fell to his knees, yet his finger kept squeezing the trigger until a dark veil shut out the light.

The gunfire stopped as suddenly as it had started. In silence the attackers approached the bodies. The smell of blood, of death, hung like a pall in the humid air.

"Take their weapons, and give me their papers and valuables," the commander said to the four heavily armed men with him. "Make it look like they were attacked by bandits."

"I don't like robbing the dead. It's—"

"Do it, soldier. That's an order. And be quick about it. We have an hour to rendezvous with the chopper."

Swallowing hard, the young soldier bent over the leader of the ambushed group. "Even him? El Lobo?" he asked.

"Especially him."

"I thought he was one of your—"

"Do it. I didn't hire you to think."

The man obeyed the gringo commander's order with a sullen expression. When he reached the woman, he shook his head. "She sure was pretty. What a waste." He ripped the golden chain with its oval locket from her neck and pulled the wedding band from her finger.

Next to her body lay a birdcage. He nudged it with one boot, but the blood-covered bird did not respond. The soldier was turning away when he heard the baby's cry.

"Madre de Dios!" he whispered, making the sign of the cross. Moving the woman's body, he saw the infant. "Commander, the baby's alive!"

"Shoot it."

"No!"

The commander glowered at the baby-faced soldier. Then he shrugged. "It would be more merciful to shoot it than to leave it to die out here, but suit yourself."

The soldier remained by the baby's side until the commander gave the order to move out. Then, furtively, in a gesture he knew was completely illogical, he dropped his water canteen next to the baby.

The thin wail of the infant pursued him for a little while before the dense vegetation of the jungle stilled it.

Chapter One

Texas

The moment Jane Peterson caught sight of the man approaching the house, her gaze darted to the closet where she kept a loaded shotgun. He had that kind of look about him.

From behind the latched screen door she watched him walk toward her. Although he looked every bit as dusty as the battered, rusty jeep he had parked by the hitching post, his steps were energetic, his posture determined. A man with a mission. Jane braced herself.

The straps of his backpack flattened the faded blue work shirt against his broad chest. Though he was dressed in the universal outfit of a cowboy, including scuffed boots and a well-worn black Stetson, something set him apart from the cowboys she had employed over the years. Jane couldn't put her finger on what it was.

"Mrs. Peterson?" The man touched his right hand politely to his hat. In his left he carried a dome-shaped object that was covered with a piece of unbleached muslin.

"I'm Jane Peterson," she said, her voice a little rusty from lack of use.

"Father Anselmo sent me. He said you were looking for a hired hand."

Another of the good father's lost sheep, but for a change this one didn't look weak, sick, or noticeably frightened. On the contrary. He looked like a man in his prime: midthirties, strong, tough as leather, with an expression on his face that was as unyielding as the Texas sun beating down on him. Perhaps the man sensed her apprehension. Before she could say anything, he spoke again.

"The padre said you should call him. He'll vouch for me."

If Father Anselmo was willing to vouch for the man, there wouldn't be anything seriously wrong with him. Jane knew that from past experience. She also knew that, despite the priest's legendary compassionate, loving nature, he was an unerringly shrewd judge of character. "What's your name?"

"Call me Santiago. Is the job still open?"

"Yes, but I doubt it's one you'd be interested in."

"Why do you say that?"

His voice had taken on a challenging edge. Although it was on the tip of Jane's tongue to blurt out that the job wasn't exciting enough, and that within two weeks' time he would be bored out of his skull with it and leave, she restrained herself.

"The job doesn't pay much," she said. "It doesn't include fancy benefits or a pension plan."

Santiago nodded. "Father Anselmo told me that."

"The place is isolated and too far from town for a quick trip to the Red Slipper Saloon for a cold beer . . . and company." When he didn't say anything, she added, "Most men find the ranch too lonely. They don't stay."

"I'm not most men."

That, undoubtedly, was an understatement. Jane watched him raise a thumb to push the Stetson back an inch or two. When she met his gaze, she blinked. With the brim of the hat pushed back, she could see his eyes clearly. They were startlingly light-colored against the sunburned skin of his face and the black hair that curled below the hat. She thought that the gaze of those pale eyes could cut through glass—or through a woman's defenses. A slight shiver whispered across her back. She was about to tell him that she couldn't hire him when a loud, complaining squawk from the dome-shaped object in his hand made her jump back.

"What was that?"

"I'm sorry. Paco likes to get in on all conversations." Santiago removed the cloth. "Paco, say hello to Mrs. Peterson."

"Hello," the bird said, tilting his head to one side.

"He's beautiful! He's every bit as spectacular as the Froot Loops bird."

"The fruit loops bird?" Santiago asked with a puzzled frown.

Now Jane realized what had been nagging at her. Though his English was faultless, every so often she caught a slight difference, an unexpected inflection, in his speech. "Where are you from, Mr. Santiago?"

"Just Santiago, please. What gave me away? Not knowing who the fruit loops bird is?"

"That and the fact that you don't aspirate the *p* in Peterson and Paco as much as native-born speakers do."

Santiago nodded. "I'll remember that." When he saw her waiting expression, he said, "I am from Guatemala, and I have papers."

"Papers," the bird repeated, and he turned in his cage.

Jane was about to ask for the papers when she saw the bird's left side. "What happened to his wing?"

"It got shot off. But he has learned to adjust his balance and doesn't fall off his perch anymore."

"How on earth did he get his wing shot off?"

"In an ambush."

Jane tried to keep her mouth from dropping open. Santiago's expression was as noncommittal as if he had made an idle comment about the weather. For a fleeting instant, his matter-of-fact reference to danger reminded her of her late husband and caused the familiar leap of anxiety. Was Santiago another male who loved the adrenaline rush of danger? Whether the danger came in the form of wild bulls in the rodeo arena or bullets or adulterous affairs didn't seem to matter to these men. She had sworn at Roy's grave that she would never again get involved with a man who courted danger. Not that she would get involved with Santiago, even if she hired him, but—

"About the job?" he prompted.

That brought Jane back to her main problem. She needed

help desperately. She couldn't run the ranch single-handedly, and ever since mysterious incidents had started to plague the ranch, she had trouble keeping hired hands. She allowed her gaze to flick over Santiago again.

He wasn't overly tall, but he looked strong and fit, with the kind of muscled body that pumping iron in a gym never produced. He wasn't exactly handsome but supremely masculine, she realized with a start, and her heart raced faster. Why was she even noticing what he looked like, and, worse, why was she feeling defensive about noticing? Was Father Anselmo right when he claimed she had lived alone too long?

"Mrs. Peterson?"

Knowing he was waiting for an answer, she asked, "Have you worked on a ranch before?"

After a tiny pause he said, "I'm good with horses." He inclined his head toward the corral, where two dozen horses watched them with curious eyes.

She could use a man who knew horses, even if he looked like trouble. On second thought, perhaps his looks were misleading. A man who cared enough about a one-winged macaw to tote him along might be harmless and gentle. Glancing at Santiago's face again, she decided that the word *harmless* was probably inappropriate. Still, he might not get drunk on Saturday nights and take the saloon apart and need to be bailed out of jail on Sunday morning. Besides, she didn't see a long line of applicants clamoring for the job.

Nor had the evasiveness of Santiago's answer escaped her. He hadn't said he had worked on a ranch. Merely that he knew horses. Not that this was much of a ranch anymore, she reflected bitterly. She was more than capable of taking care of the few head of cattle she still owned, but she did need help with the horses.

A whimpering sound from the direction of his backpack caused Jane to exclaim, "That sounded like a baby!"

"It was." The whimper grew louder. "May I?" he asked, lowering the cage.

Still stunned, she said, "Yes, of course. Come up onto the porch."

Santiago took the four stairs in two steps. He placed the cage on the wooden floor before he swung the backpack down gently. It had been converted into a baby sling. Quickly she unhooked the screen door and said, "Come on in." She couldn't leave a man and a baby standing in the blazing noonday sun of a Texas summer day, not even if the man had *Jack the Ripper* stenciled on his forehead.

"She's really a good baby, but I suspect she's hungry, hot, and needs changing," Santiago explained with a hint of apology in his voice.

"I don't have any baby food." How dumb of her to say that. Father Anselmo had undoubtedly told him that she was widowed and childless, so Santiago wouldn't expect her to have a few jars of Gerber's tucked away in her pantry.

"If you could hold her a minute, I'll get what we need from the jeep."

Before Jane could protest that she knew little about babies, Santiago had thrust the infant into her arms and rushed out the door. Her arms tightened protectively around the small body that fit her arms so naturally, so perfectly. Something frozen shifted inside her.

"Well, it's just you and me, baby girl," Jane murmured. Instinctively she patted the baby's back and started pacing. Apparently the infant found the motion soothing, for she stopped crying. "Oh, you like that," Jane said, absurdly pleased by the baby's response.

Jane kept pacing and crooning to the baby until Santiago returned, carrying a duffel bag and a large plastic sack. He paused in the long hallway, uncertain where to go.

"We'd better use the spare room." Jane led the way. "The bathroom's right next door," she said, gesturing. Quickly Jane crossed to the nearest window. "I keep the shutters closed during the noon hours to keep the house cool," she explained. She opened one of the wooden shutters.

Although every other week she dusted the maple furniture and mopped the painted wooden floor, she hadn't really looked at the room in ages, hadn't noticed how sparse, almost spartan, it was with its two single beds, chest of drawers, and lone ladder-back chair in a corner. The only decorative item, her great-grandmother's round mirror with its intricately carved frame, hung on the wall. Though plain, the room was clean.

"It's not fancy. Nothing on the ranch is," she said. Jane couldn't believe that her voice had sounded almost apologetic. If she wasn't careful, she'd be apologizing next for not wearing makeup and perfume.

"This is more than fine," Santiago said. He removed the Stetson and placed it on the chair.

At first Jane thought he'd merely parted his hair crookedly, but then she noticed the scar that started high on his forehead and continued on into his thick black hair. Something had permanently parted his hair. Something like a bullet or a blade. Jane's heart lurched. Maybe she'd been overly hasty in inviting this man into her house.

She watched him place a plastic square on the bed. When he took the baby from her, Jane's arms felt achingly empty.

The baby gurgled happily. The look in Santiago's pale, tawny eyes and the smile that softened his sculpted features reassured her. A man who could look at a baby with such pure affection and tenderness couldn't be all bad.

Santiago removed the baby's pink sunbonnet.

"What a lot of dark hair she has." Jane reached out to touch the baby's head. "And her hair is softer than silk. How old is she?"

"She's six months old."

Bending over the baby, Jane said softly, "You're a pretty little girl, aren't you?"

"She looks like her mother."

"Where is her mother?" She could feel the tension slam into him. The smile died on his face. *Great going, Jane.* She had been around horses and cattle so long, she had lost whatever people skills she'd had.

"Her mother is dead."

"I'm sorry."

"So am I."

The way he uttered the three simple words told her more eloquently than a long speech would have how painful it was for him to speak of his wife's death. There was nothing she could say to make him feel better. She knew that from personal experience. All the condolences at her husband's funeral hadn't lessened her grief or her anger. Her heart went out to Santiago in sympathy. And to the baby—especially to the baby. To lose a mother at so tender an age that the baby wouldn't even remember her was heartbreakingly cruel.

Jane's throat was so tight, she couldn't speak for several seconds. Finally she asked, "What's the baby's name?"

"Marisa."

"That's a lovely name." When the baby squirmed on the bed, Jane asked, "What can I do to help?"

"If you wouldn't mind, you could warm one of those jars of meat-and-vegetables while I change her diaper."

She must have looked puzzled, or he guessed that she had little experience with babies, for he added that the simplest way to do that was to place the jar into a pan of hot water. Jane took a jar of chicken-vegetable food from the sack. In the hall she picked up the birdcage and took it to the kitchen with her. While the food warmed in a pan, the phone rang.

"I thought it would be you, Father Anselmo," Jane said, after he'd uttered no more than a simple greeting.

"Ah. So Santiago and the baby arrived at the ranch."

"Yes."

"Jane, do you have any questions?"

"I have a tubful of questions. What happened to the baby's mother? How did he get that scar? What did he—"

"You have to ask him about all that."

"Don't you know?"

"I do, but I can't discuss his private life."

"Father, you're doing it again! You're always doing this to me. Hinting at something and then clamming up. Why do you ask me if I have questions when you have no intention of answering them?"

"I meant, do you have any questions about his character, about his trustworthiness. Things that bear on hiring him to work for you."

"Are you telling me he isn't trustworthy?"

"Of course not. I wouldn't have sent Santiago to you if I thought that."

"Then I have no questions. Besides, a man who treats a baby and a one-winged bird with such loving care must have a few redeeming qualities."

"Santiago is a good man." Then Father Anselmo chuckled. "I don't know about that bird, though. His vocabulary is a little racy."

"So far he's behaved himself."

"Paco isn't stupid. He'll wait until he's won you over before he uses his more colorful words."

Jane looked at the bird speculatively.

"What did Santiago say when you offered him the job?"

"I haven't offered it to him yet."

"But you will."

That this was a statement rather than a question bothered her. Was she that predictable? "How can you be so sure of that?" Jane challenged.

"I've known you all your life. I baptized you when you were three days old. That was twenty-nine years ago."

"Thirty, father. I just had a birthday. One of these days I'll do something you won't expect."

"Well, then. All's settled. You needed a hired hand, and Santiago needed a home."

"But there's more to your Good Samaritan deed, isn't there?"

"Yes. I'm worried about you," Father Anselmo said.

"I'm safe here on the ranch."

"It's not your physical safety I'm worried about."

"You're worried about my spiritual state?"

"No. You're a woman of strong faith. It's your emotional

well-being that worries me. You know that poem about no person being an island?"

"I do, but I don't understand where you're headed with this," Jane said, not wanting to go where he was leading her.

"You know what I'm talking about. You're withdrawing more and more from human contact. The time between your visits to town grows longer and longer. That much isolation isn't good for anyone. We'll talk again soon, but now you'd better get back to Santiago. Peace be with you, Jane."

Could Father Anselmo be right? She had been going less and less often into town but had attributed that to the work she had to do. In part that was true. There was always more work than she could complete in one day. On the other hand, she also had little desire to see people. Well, if she hired Santiago, she wouldn't be alone anymore.

If she hired him?

With a start Jane realized that it really was settled. She didn't know exactly when she had decided to hire Santiago, but she had. Even more startling was the discovery that she had made that decision before the padre's phone call.

The enormity of her decision hit her. She had decided to hire a man about whom she knew next to nothing. A man who had secrets. Probably dangerous secrets. Who hadn't told her the whole truth.

Well, everybody had secrets, and nobody revealed everything. Including her. Besides, the hands she had hired who had presented her with references hadn't always worked out so well either. The last two had hightailed it off the ranch at the first sign of trouble. By the look of him, Santiago just might be made from sterner stuff.

And then there was the baby. The sweet little girl had lost her mother. Jane felt such tenderness rise in her chest that it almost robbed her of her breath. She had wanted a baby of her own so badly, but Roy kept saying that they had lots of time to start a family. He'd been wrong. Hearing a sound behind her, she whirled around. Santiago stood in the doorway, the baby nestled against his shoulder.

"I didn't mean to startle you," he said.

"You certainly don't make much noise when you move." He had tied a bib around the baby's neck. He carried a small spoon and a baby bottle. Placing both items on the table, Santiago sat down.

Jane took the jar from the warm water and handed it to him. In doing so, she accidentally touched his hand. The unexpected contact startled her so that she jerked her hand away and hastily shoved it into the pocket of her jeans. The man made her as jumpy as a herd of cattle in a thunderstorm.

"Would you set the bottle into the pan, please?"

Jane took her time doing that. "I have half a gallon of milk in the refrigerator, if you need it for Marisa."

"Thanks, but I have a carton of formula."

Jane watched him spoon the pureed food into the baby's eager mouth. He had obviously done this many times, for his movements were deft and skilled. For the first time, she noticed his hands—and they did not look like hands that were used to gripping a shovel or a pitchfork. He must have noticed her stare. His left eyebrow arched. Quickly she said, "Judging by the way Marisa is eating, she really was hungry."

"She's not a fussy eater. If she had been, she wouldn't have survived."

Jane waited for Santiago to explain, but his suddenly somber, closed expression told her that he wouldn't. Surprised, she discovered that she wanted him to confide in her. *Why?* She was a solitary person herself who kept her own counsel, so why was she so eager to know all about this man?

She watched him get up to fetch the bottle, test the milk's warmth on his wrist, and place the nipple in the baby's mouth. She admired the way he took care of the baby. He noticed her watching him.

"What is it you want to ask me?"

"I didn't mean to stare. I'm impressed by the way you take care of Marisa. I wouldn't know how."

"We do what we have to do," he said simply.

Jane understood that only too well. She, too, did what she

had to do. Her admiration for this quiet man ratcheted up another rung. Santiago was well-mannered and soft-spoken. Where had he learned the English language? Except for the occasional faintly accented word, he could pass for an American. An educated American. What sort of life had he led in Guatemala? Or, more important, since leaving that country?

"Have you made a decision about hiring me?" he asked.

"Yes. The job's yours if you want it."

"I'll take it. Thank you."

"Don't be too quick to thank me. The work's hard, the hours long, and the pay short."

"I understand that, Mrs. Peterson."

"Call me Jane, please."

"Thank you, Jane." He paused for a moment before he spoke again. "You've probably wondered how I'm going to take care of Marisa and work for you. I can't give you an uninterrupted workday." He paused for her reaction.

"That's okay. Ranchers don't punch a time clock."

Santiago nodded. "My schedule follows hers. After she's finished this bottle, she'll sleep for a solid three hours. I'll put her in the baby buggy that Father Anselmo borrowed from one of his parishioners and take her with me to where you want me to work. When she wakes up, she'll need a little attention, but then she'll be quite content to watch me until supper time. We follow a similar schedule in the morning. Is that acceptable?"

"Yes. You'll do your own laundry, and I'll fix the meals. But I have to warn you that I'm not a fancy cook."

"I'm no cook at all, so whatever you prepare will be fine. Where will Marisa and I sleep? In the bunkhouse?"

"Good heavens, no!" Envisioning the baby in the bunkhouse, with its stale, foul smell of tobacco that no amount of airing out could eliminate, Jane repressed a shudder. No telling what harm the lingering remnants of tobacco smoke might do to a baby's delicate lungs. "The bunkhouse won't do. Not for the baby."

She examined the alternatives. The ranch house had been

built at a time when the area was still a frontier. Back then four large rooms were considered adequate, if not luxurious, for a family's needs, and, oddly enough, none of the subsequent tenants had added anything except electricity, a bathroom, and kitchen appliances.

She couldn't put the baby in the bunkhouse. Given that, it was obvious that she had no choice but to share her house with this man. He would sleep in the room next to her bedroom. For an instant a tiny flutter of alarm surged through her before she reminded herself that the baby would, of course, share the room with him. She would be a small but powerful deterrent to any wayward impulses. At least she hoped so. Then another alarming thought hit her.

What if Santiago thought that placing him next to her room might be an invitation to . . . Surely he couldn't think that. Until a few weeks ago the thought wouldn't have occurred to her either. Then, during the deputy sheriff's last visit, he had let her know, smirking, that a woman who was entering her thirties and living alone in the boondocks should be grateful for any male attention, even his. Or especially his. Jane had been sorely tempted to order Bud Wilson off her land, but, unfortunately, he represented the law, which she needed. Gritting her teeth, she had thanked him for his concern but had politely declined to take him up on his offer. He hadn't liked her refusal. She had the sick foreboding that that wasn't the end of her problems with him, but in the context of all her other troubles, he seemed no more than a minor irritant.

Jane stole a look at the man holding the baby. Unlike that underworked and overweight deputy, Santiago looked like a man who had known his share of grief and problems. Surely he had more important things on his mind than her lack of male companionship. It would be all right. Jane took a calming breath.

She glanced at Santiago, who was obviously waiting for an answer. With as much composure as she could manage, she repeated, "The bunkhouse is unsuitable, so I think you and the baby had better use the spare room."

"Thank you. I appreciate that." Santiago studied Jane's face for a moment. "Just to put your mind at ease, Jane, let me assure you that I was raised to treat women with respect and consideration. You'll be quite safe."

"I never thought I wouldn't be safe," she maintained, a little stung by his accurate assessment of her momentary doubt. "I'm no longer so young that I think the fact that I am a woman is reason enough for any man to want me."

"I didn't mean to suggest that you are not an attractive woman. Merely that I'm no longer so young that my hormones would drive me to seduction."

His voice, with that appealing hint of an accent, was warm and low and pleasing. "Well, then, since we're both old enough to behave in a responsible manner, there's no reason for you not to take the spare room."

"Are you sure this will not damage your reputation?"

His question rendered her speechless. She couldn't remember the last time a man had worried about trashing her reputation.

"If staying in the spare room presents a problem—"

"It doesn't." Jane rallied her thoughts. "Not many people come to the ranch. So unless you intend to broadcast the fact that you're living in the main house, probably no one will find out." Jane shrugged. "And if they do? Well, I'm also old enough not to care a whole lot if I'm gossiped about."

Chapter Two

Santiago moved the buggy far enough into the barn that the sun wouldn't hit the baby's face. Marisa was sound asleep, one tiny fist pressed against her mouth. Three months ago in that jungle clearing he had almost given up hope for her survival, and look at her now.

She was a fighter, just like her mother. Like all the women in his family. The memory of Corazon, of how she had died, fueled his barely banked anger, further hardening his already rock-hard resolution. It was up to him to find a way for Marisa to grow up fine and strong—and in this country. In Guatemala the family had too many enemies with long, merciless memories. He had to find a way for them to stay in the United States. And he would. Just as he would find a way to settle the score with the people who had betrayed him.

Hearing Jane working in the back stall, Santiago picked up his pitchfork and went to work.

"Is the baby asleep?" she asked him.

"Yes. Thanks for the boots," he said, pointing to the Wellington-style boots he was wearing.

"Some cowboys think it's sacrilegious to wear rubber boots, but why wear leather to muck out stalls? You can take a hose and run water over the rubber boots, and they're clean. No scraping, polishing, or shining."

"Makes sense to me," Santiago agreed. Jane struck him as a woman who preferred efficiency to tradition and did things her own way. Still, judging by her earlier reaction, she wasn't quite as indifferent to public opinion as she thought she was. Being a proud woman, she would mind gossip about her private

16

life. He liked pride and self-respect in a woman. He also liked that she didn't feel the need to chatter but was comfortable with silence.

As they worked side by side, Santiago kept glancing at her. What had first struck him about Jane was the intelligence and empathy he had glimpsed in her cinnamon-brown eyes. Now, with each look, he discovered something else about her. Jane's beauty wasn't flashy or obvious. Measured by contemporary standards, most people wouldn't consider her beautiful at all, and yet hers was the kind of face that would capture a man's eyes again and again.

Jane intercepted one of his assessing glances and frowned. He couldn't let her catch him staring at her. Quickly he asked, "How long have you been taking care of the place by yourself?"

"Almost a month now."

Astonished, Santiago paused to look at her. "You've been taking care of all those horses and the house and the cattle all by yourself?"

"I didn't have a choice. The people who board their horses with me expect me to take care of them. That's what they pay me for."

"Who are these people who board their horses with you?"

"Some are from town, but most of these horses belong to city people who come out here once or twice a month to ride, camp out, and rough it. It's part of your job to help when they come." Jane shot him an assessing look.

"That's fine," Santiago assured her.

Before he could help her, Jane had swung a bale of straw onto the clean floor of the stall, cut the twine, and started to spread it around. Her slenderness was deceptive. She was stronger than she looked. She had to be, to do the hard, physical work the ranch demanded. His admiration for her crept up another notch.

"Usually I muck out the stalls first thing in the morning," she explained, her tone apologetic, "but someone was up on the mesa last night, so I rode up there to look around and check on the cattle."

"How do you know someone was up there?"

"I saw lights and heard noises."

"What kind of noises?"

"The noise of an engine. Or engines." When she saw his startled look, she added, "Yes, I know. Why should any kind of engine be up there? No one lives on the mesa. Nor is it a convenient shortcut to anywhere."

"Have you heard these engine noises before?"

"Yes."

"Did you find anything up there?"

"No. But I'm not a tracker, and the earth is very hard, since it hasn't rained in months." Jane shrugged apologetically. "Before my last two hands quit, I sent them up there to have a look around."

"What did they find?" Santiago asked.

"That's hard to say. One of them thought he saw evil spirits or ghosts. The other maintained it was men from outer space with glowing eyes on their foreheads." Jane shrugged. "I suspect they had a bottle along, but whatever it was they saw, it scared them enough to quit on the spot. They didn't even wait for the couple of days' worth of wages I owed them."

Santiago stared thoughtfully at the ground. "What's the terrain like up there?"

"Flat. And now very dry." Jane shook her head. Exasperated, she said, "It's just a large, flat plateau. I can't imagine what reason anyone could have for being up there."

Santiago could think of at least one reason. If he was right, and he was 99 percent sure that he was, that reason would cause a lot of trouble. Trouble he looked forward to, trouble he was aching to take on and settle once and for all.

Jane paced the length of the porch. Shifting the baby so she could look at her wristwatch, she noted with alarm how much time had passed since Santiago left. She stared at the mountains. Where was he?

He had left for the high mesa hours ago. Had something happened to him? Jane shook her head, trying to suppress that worrisome thought. In the two weeks he had been at the ranch, he had demonstrated that he was both resourceful and capable. Still, the terrain was rough, and an accident could happen to anyone at any time.

When the baby fussed, she resumed pacing, wondering if Marisa sensed the anxiety Jane tried to hide.

"What's the matter, baby girl?" she crooned. "You've been fussy all day." Jane slid a hand under the baby's shirt to feel the skin between her shoulder blades. "No fever, I think," she murmured, relieved. Still, something was wrong with Marisa. What could it be? Before she could worry what else might be upsetting the baby, the telephone rang. Jane dashed into the kitchen to answer it.

It was Father Anselmo. They exchanged greetings while the baby squirmed and fussed in her arms.

"What's wrong with Marisa?" Father Anselmo asked.

"I'm not sure," Jane said, close to tears. "She's been cranky and unhappy all day." Jane recited all the symptoms she had looked for. "I can't see anything physically wrong with her, except she drools a lot and chews on everything I let her get ahold of. Right now she's gnawing on the collar of my blouse. I don't know what to do—"

"Relax, Jane. Sounds like she's teething."

"Teething? I never thought of that," Jane admitted, feeling enormously relieved. "I wonder how parents survive raising their first child without suffering a nervous breakdown."

The padre chuckled. Then, growing serious, he asked, "Is that all that's worrying you?"

Jane was tempted to give an evasive answer but changed her mind. The padre always got the truth out of her eventually.

"Santiago rode up to the mesa hours ago. He should have been back by now."

"He can take care of himself," Father Anselmo said, as calm as if he'd been saying a prayer. "There's no reason for you to worry."

"I thought I'd wait another hour and then call the neighbors. I'm sure one of their girls can watch the baby while I ride out to look for him. You know how rough the terrain is. He might have gotten lost." Jane didn't add her fear that Santiago might be hurt.

"I wouldn't worry about him getting lost. At least not literally."

"What do you mean by that?" Jane asked.

"Nothing, nothing. Have you informed the sheriff of the lights on the mesa?"

"Yes, but he hasn't bothered to come to check it out."

"Jane, be fair. The man has a large territory to cover."

"Father, you always see the positive in every person and in every situation."

"That's my job. At least part of it. Have Santiago call me when he gets back." Sensing her anxiety, he added, "Or call me if he isn't back by six. I'll drive out to the ranch."

Santiago rubbed down the horse he'd ridden before he headed for the house, the shotgun cradled in the crook of his right arm.

As always, the front door of the ranch house was unlocked. He'd have to persuade Jane to keep it locked from now on. And replace the old lock. He set the shotgun in the corner of the closet where Jane kept it. He was about to call out her name when he heard her softly crooning, appealing voice. He had come to look forward to hearing her voice. Low, a little throaty, it could lure a man to his destruction or his salvation. Santiago followed the siren voice to the bedroom he shared with the baby.

The door was partially open. He lifted a hand to push it open wider. He didn't know what kept him from doing that, but what he saw left him standing there as if rooted to the floor. Jane, still singing a lullaby, tried to tug the collar of her blouse out of the baby's tiny fists. Each time she tried, Marisa fussed and whimpered. Jane soothed her until she fell asleep again. Finally, Jane unbuttoned the blouse, shrugged out of it carefully and a little awkwardly, and laid both the blouse and the baby into the baby buggy.

Santiago felt his throat tighten. Who'd have thought that

beneath the loose shirts she wore Jane hid such a lovely body? His heartbeat accelerated. When he became aware of it, he berated himself. What was wrong with him? Jane had given him a job and a home, a chance to stay in this great country. She treated the baby as if she were her own, and he, instead of thinking of her only as his generous employer and saintly benefactor, saw her as a desirable woman.

He took several silent steps backward before he cleared his throat and approached the bedroom. Jane, with her back to him, struggled to slip into the shirt he'd tossed onto the bed that morning. He stopped and waited for her to turn around.

She did, a blush covering her face. Jane signaled him to keep quiet and tiptoed out of the bedroom. He closed the door behind them and followed her to the kitchen.

"Marisa is teething. Chewing on my blouse soothed her. I took your shirt. Hope you don't mind."

"I don't mind." From her short, choppy statements he guessed she was embarrassed. She probably wondered if he'd seen her without her blouse on. Jane was a modest woman.

"I could use some iced tea. How about you?" she asked.

"Yes, thank you. I had a long, hot ride."

"I'm afraid we're out of lemons. We need to drive into town soon." She took a sip of tea. Then she looked at him expectantly. "What did you find on the mesa?"

"You were right. The ground's too hard and dry for tracks." Seeing her disappointed expression, he added quickly, "But I did find something. Several drops of oil. The kind used in motors."

"Oh."

She seemed disappointed. He hated to disappoint her.

"Leanne told me that they leave the jeeps on the little plateau just below the mesa," Jane mused aloud.

"Who is Leanne?" Santiago asked.

"Leanne Jessup. She's my high school friend. Remember the camping parties I mentioned when I hired you? She's in charge of setting up camp and doing everything to make the guests comfortable but still give them the illusion that they're roughing it. Maybe someone in the party found a way to drive the jeeps all the way up the mesa. That would account for the motor oil."

Santiago shook his head. "The grade is too steep for any jeep to make it."

"So what are you saying? That the oil is from . . . ?"

"A small plane. At least that's what I suspect."

She nodded her head thoughtfully. "I wondered if the lights and the noise could belong to a plane. I just wasn't sure one could land on the mesa." She drank some tea before she spoke again. "Mexico's on the other side of the mountains. What could a plane be delivering or picking up? People? Illegals?"

Santiago shook his head again. "A plane that can land on the mesa is too small to make smuggling people profitable. Also, the people would have to pass too close to your place. Or your neighbors'. They could be spotted too easily."

"What, then?"

"Drugs would be my guess." He watched her cinnamon eyes widen in dismay.

"Drugs," she repeated, her voice a hoarse whisper. Jane jumped up, too agitated to sit still.

Santiago touched her arm to make her stop pacing. She looked at him, her eyes filled with misery. "Jane, what did you think was happening on the mesa?"

"I don't know. I suspected everything from secret government activities to terrorists, to people smuggling, to my ranch hands' 'ghosts,' to . . ." Jane shook her head. "I did wonder about drugs." She took a deep breath. "What kind of drugs?"

Santiago shrugged. "Several weeks ago there was an article in the newspaper about drug smuggling along the border. You remember it?"

Jane shook her head. "I only see the newspaper when I go to town. What did it say?"

"They interviewed one of the border patrol officers. He said that along *la frontera,* marijuana was the contraband they most often confiscated."

Jane shook her head again, as if wanting to deny everything

she heard. "Maybe we're wrong about the smuggling. Maybe there's a logical explanation for everything."

"Maybe," he conceded.

"But you don't think so."

"I don't know. We have no proof one way or another."

"I think I'll phone the sheriff again. Or, better yet, why don't I find out the number of the nearest office of the Drug Enforcement Agency and have them come and investigate?"

"No!"

Taken aback by his emphatic reply, Jane looked at him through slightly narrowed eyes. "You don't want me to phone the DEA? Why not?"

"Now you're wondering if I'm involved in drug smuggling. Jane, I swear to you. I am not running drugs. I have never dealt in drugs. Never. The reason I don't want you to contact the DEA is that the sheriff will resent your going over his head. As isolated as you are out here, it seems to me you'd want to be on good terms with the sheriff in case of trouble. Don't you?"

"Yes," she admitted.

"Besides, we have absolutely no proof that anything illegal is going on. At least not yet."

"I hate not doing anything."

"I do too, but I think for right now we wait. When's the next camping party due?" he asked.

"This weekend. But that's Susan Baldwin's party. She owns department stores and oil wells and banks and heaven only knows what else. She couldn't possibly be involved in anything shady."

"She doesn't come alone, does she?"

"No, there's . . . I see what you mean. It could be one of her guests. Maybe we should speak with Leanne. Ask her—"

"No," Santiago said, his voice firm.

"But I've known Leanne most of my life. She's a single mom, works hard, goes to church—"

"For the time being, we'd better not say anything to anybody. You informed the sheriff. Let him do his job."

Jane hesitated for a beat and then nodded.

"I'd better go and exercise the horses. Especially the roan. He's frisky. We can't have him throw one of the guests this weekend," Santiago said.

"Oh, I almost forgot. Father Anselmo phoned. He wants you to call him back. I'll start exercising the horses."

By noon on Friday, Jane took one last look around to be sure everything was ready for the weekend campers. It should be. She and Santiago had been up since four thirty. She adjusted the flower-sprigged tablecloth on the long picnic table that straddled the center of the tent. Santiago joined her.

"The horses look good," he said, with a proud glance at the corral. "And the stables are clean, the feed sacks are ready, and the water barrel is filled."

Jane nodded, pleased. "The charcoal is just about ready for whatever Leanne is barbecuing." Jane picked up a pot holder and checked the contents of the blue-enameled pot. "Coffee's about ready too, though it'll probably be just us and Leanne drinking it. If it's Susan's usual crowd, they'll be having imported beer and margaritas."

"Do you need me to help with lunch?"

"No. Just help Leanne unload her stuff." He seemed relieved. "I help with the food. Let's go sit down until they arrive." Jane pushed the baby buggy to the porch and sat on the middle step. Santiago checked on Marisa before he sat beside Jane, his thigh almost touching hers.

"Marisa's still asleep. If she wakes up, I'll take care of her." Idly, he asked, "Who are these people who want to rough it for a weekend?"

"I told you about Susan. She's one of the richest women in Texas. The people she invites to these outings are businessmen, lawyers, politicians, and their wives or girlfriends. Occasionally she even brings a movie star."

"You don't sound terribly impressed."

Jane shot him a quick look. "To tell you the truth, if I didn't need the money Susan pays me, I wouldn't bother. This is a working ranch, not a dude ranch catering to people pretending to be cowboys."

"The myth of the Wild West is powerful stuff."

'Myth' is right. If they had to live real ranch life for more than a day, they'd hightail it back to town so fast, they'd get there before the dust had a chance to settle."

Santiago laughed. Startled, Jane looked at him. He smiled at Marisa and occasionally at her, but she'd never heard him laugh. She liked the sound of his laughter. And the laugh crinkles around his mesmerizing eyes, which were the color of sweet honey. Something about his eyes kept tugging at her memory but vanished before the image could surface into her consciousness.

Santiago leaned back, his forearms resting on the top step, his long legs stretched out, totally at ease. In the process of rearranging his body, his thigh pressed against hers. The warmth from his body sizzled straight into her bloodstream, causing her breath to catch and her heart to beat fast. Jane almost leaped to her feet to escape this disquieting, disturbing male touch. No, not just any male's touch—Santiago's touch. If any other man had sat that close to her, she'd have slanted him a cold look and put more space between them. With Santiago, she remained seated, her body accepting the heat from his, her pulse racing.

"That dust cloud?" he asked, pointing. "Is it—?"

"Yes." And the camping party had arrived not a moment too soon. Jane jumped up and walked toward the tent.

Santiago lifted the baby carriage onto the porch before he followed Jane. They watched a long column of jeeps, pickups, SUVs, and horse trailers come to a halt in the yard.

Santiago muttered something under his breath. Then in a low tone he added, "Why do they bother to come out here? They've brought every luxury with them."

Jane chuckled. "If you have enough money, you can do all sorts of outlandish and foolish things. Let's go help Leanne. She looks stressed out and hot."

At the pickup they usually referred to as the chuck wagon, Jane introduced Santiago to Leanne and her assistant. Byron Jones was young, probably just a year or two past the legal drinking age, good-looking in a pouty, sulking sort of way, and supremely confident in his appeal to women. Every time he came with Leanne, Jane was surprised that he was still working for her. She had seen his type on the rodeo circuit, where they looked for women who'd pick up tabs in bars and motels, not for broncos to bust. Was Leanne . . . *no.* Jane quickly dismissed the disloyal thought. Leanne wouldn't stoop to keeping a man. Besides, she had two children to support.

"The blue cooler contains the drinks," Jane told Santiago. "Could you carry it to the smallest table?" She picked up two wicker baskets and took them to the worktable.

"What are we serving today?" she asked Leanne.

"Barbecued beef on sourdough buns." Leanne set a large pot over the coals. "I just have to heat the meat and grill the buns."

"I can do that." Jane buttered buns and put them around the edges of the grill to toast. While she did that, she studied Susan's guests, wondering if any of them could be involved in drug smuggling.

Susan joined her. "That hunk over there. Who is he?"

Deliberately misunderstanding her, Jane said, "Byron Jones. Leanne's assistant."

"No, not that boy. I mean the man. The one who looks like masculinity personified."

"You mean my hired hand, Santiago?"

"If hired hands look like that, I'm going to buy me a ranch real fast," Susan drawled, and she sauntered toward Santiago, who was helping Leanne set out salads and side dishes.

Jane tried to keep her eyes on the buns, but her glance kept straying to Susan and Santiago, who were walking toward the corral. Leave it to Susan to find a quick angle to engage the man she'd set her sights on. Telling herself that Santiago couldn't very well refuse to discuss the horses Susan was boarding at the ranch, Jane focused on the task before her.

Masculinity personified. Susan had unerringly hit on the

perfect description of Santiago. He wasn't as handsome as Byron, but there probably wasn't a woman around who wouldn't respond to that strong, confident, manly quality in Santiago, and it would be him they'd turn to for help and comfort.

Comfort, though, wasn't what Susan was angling for. The way she tossed that expensively styled and highlighted hair, the way she leaned toward him when speaking to him, the way she casually touched his arm . . . all of it annoyed Jane. Though she tried telling herself that she had no claim on Santiago and that he could flirt with any woman who caught his fancy, it didn't calm her down.

By the time Leanne rang the triangle to summon the guests to the table, Jane was thoroughly irritated. Her reaction surprised her. She hadn't been this riled up since the early days of her marriage, when rodeo groupies pursued and frequently captured her husband's attention.

Fortunately for her temper, she was kept busy dispensing drinks and food. When she looked toward the corral, Santiago had disappeared. Alarmed, she looked around. Susan was sitting with her guests. A quick glance at the front porch told her that Santiago had taken the baby inside.

It took a good ninety minutes for the leisurely lunch to be over, the horses coaxed into their trailers, everything repacked, and the party leaving for the site of their first campground. As soon as the last truck pulled out of the yard, Santiago joined her.

"They're finally gone. Took them long enough."

"They're in no hurry." Jane slid him a quick look. "From what I saw, you seemed to be pleasurably occupied with the group's hostess. Flirting to beat the band."

"You noticed?" he asked with a roguish grin.

"It was hard to miss."

"Well, if you looked, then you should also have noticed that she was doing all the flirting. I couldn't walk away without being rude. You told me you needed the income from these jaunts."

"I do, unfortunately."

"I hope you also noticed that I disappeared. Hid out with Marisa."

"I don't believe you'd need to hide from someone like Susan."

"Don't be too sure. That woman is so hard, a man could break his teeth on her." Santiago paused. "That wasn't a good English expression?"

"Oh, I don't know about that. It certainly was descriptive, if unusual." She couldn't help but smile.

"Good. You're not angry." Santiago looked around. "They left all this mess for us to clean up?"

"But first we eat. Aren't you hungry?" she asked.

"Starving. That barbecue smelled great."

"What about the baby?"

"Fed and put down for a nap."

Jane scooped the leftover slaw onto two plates and fixed one sandwich for herself and two for Santiago. She checked the tub they'd used to keep drinks cold.

"Darn. I hoped they'd leave a bottle of beer for you, but no such luck. Just some tomato juice."

"Juice is fine."

When they'd finished their sandwiches, Jane brought out the two pieces of cheesecake she'd set aside. She poured them two cups of coffee.

"I think we deserve this," she said, and she closed her eyes blissfully after the first forkful of cheesecake.

Santiago chuckled. Growing serious, he asked, "What do you want me to do next? Help you clean up or mend the fence in the west pasture?"

"What would you rather do?"

"Mend the fence."

"You got it," Jane said with a smile.

It took Jane the better part of the afternoon to clean up. Susan disdained paper plates and plastic forks, and though she didn't demand Lennox china and Waterford crystal, the stainless steel, earthenware, and plain glasses she asked for had to be washed, dried, and stored for the next time.

Jane carried the folding chairs into the tack room, picked up the tablecloth and napkins, and carried them to the house to be laundered. All that was left to be put away was the tent. She'd need Santiago's help to take it down.

As soon as she entered the house, she heard the baby fussing mildly. Marisa was such a good baby. She didn't cry when waking up, didn't demand immediate attention. Jane knew she had a few minutes to herself. She took a quick shower.

She didn't know what made her pause in combing the tangles out of her wet hair and look, really look, at herself in the mirror. She frowned. When was the last time she'd given her hair a deep conditioning or put a moisturizing mask on her face? Susan's meticulous appearance reminded Jane that she needed to take better care of herself. She no longer lived alone. A small sigh of relief escaped her.

She wouldn't have admitted to anyone, not even Father Anselmo, that she had been lonely, desperately lonely, until Santiago came and pushed the shadows and old ghosts into the far corners of the house. He and Marisa made her feel as if she'd awakened from a long, drugged sleep.

Would she mind if Santiago left only because he would take the baby with him? Jane, almost always ruthlessly honest with herself, admitted that she loved the baby but would also miss him, miss his tall, reassuring male presence, the smell of his aftershave in the morning, and the smell of salt and leather clinging to him in the evening after a long day's work, miss the warmth of his rare smiles and his even rarer laughter.

All right, so she'd gotten accustomed to him. A person became accustomed to everything that grew into a constant in their daily lives. No big deal. *Liar,* the small voice in her head whispered. *You'd mind terribly if he left.* Before she could examine her feelings in depth, she heard Marisa fuss.

From the kitchen, Paco squawked, "Baby. Baby. Baby."

Chapter Three

Jane awoke from an uneasy sleep. Had Marisa cried out? Barefoot, she rushed into the hall. The door to the other bedroom stood ajar. Silently she tiptoed toward it. The full moon shining through the open windows provided enough light for Jane to see that Santiago's bed was empty. Alarmed, she rushed to the baby's bed. Marisa was sleeping soundly. *Thank heaven.* She expelled the breath she'd been holding. But where was Santiago?

The slight, cool breeze she felt on her back told her that the front door was open. She knew she had locked it earlier. Jane crept through the hall and eased the front closet open. She reached for the shotgun before she stepped outside.

Santiago stood at the end of the porch, binoculars raised to his eyes. When she came closer, she saw that he wore only jeans. His chest was bare. For a moment she allowed herself to admire his wide shoulders, his trim waist, his finely muscled arms, before she looked away, afraid her hands would reach out to touch him.

"Where did you get those fancy binoculars?" she asked, her voice low.

"They're night-vision goggles," he said. Quickly he added, "I'm sorry I woke you. You're a light sleeper. I thought I moved as silently as a cat."

"More like a . . ." Her voice trailed off. Suddenly she knew what his eyes reminded her of.

"Finish the sentence, Jane. Don't keep a man dangling."

"More like a wolf."

30

As offhandedly as he could, he asked, "What about me reminds you of a wolf?"

"Your eyes. Their color. And your gaze is watchful, penetrating. You're alert to danger."

"Have you ever seen a wolf?"

"Once. Wolves are supposed to be extinct around here, but I swear I came face-to-face with one about two years ago. And it wasn't a coyote. I've seen enough of them to know that this wasn't one. He was beautiful, so don't be offended by the comparison."

He chuckled. "Nobody has called me beautiful in a long time, *querida*."

Jane knew enough Spanish to recognize the endearment. It warmed her heart.

Santiago turned around and looked at the mesa again through his goggles.

"You're expecting something to happen tonight?"

"Tonight or Sunday night. Or not at all, if this isn't the right group."

"Why not Saturday night?" she wanted to know.

"Because tomorrow night there'll be a lot of campers on the mesa. Difficult for even a small plane to land. Unless, of course, we're all wrong about the mesa's being used for criminal purposes."

"A plane could be bringing in a late camper," Jane said.

"Doubtful. Why risk a hard landing? There's no regular landing strip up there."

"I've been wondering about that. How can a pilot land a plane there? Runways are brightly marked with lights, aren't they?"

"Someone on the ground lights flares to guide the plane down."

Jane shivered, though the night was not cold. "Someone sneaks away from the party and rides up to the mesa?"

"That's my guess." Santiago looked at her. She stood beside him, wearing a simple white, sleeveless cotton gown that reached down to her ankles. He smelled the scent of her hair, her skin. Jasmine. He would have thought she'd wear the scent of flowers like lilacs, roses, or lily of the valley. On second thought, jasmine suited her. Just a hint of the exotic, the mysterious. Her quietness had depth, a depth a man like him longed to explore with exquisite slowness. Quickly he transferred his gaze to the mesa again, fighting off the impulse to kiss her.

Jane leaned the shotgun against the wall and hugged her arms around herself.

"Why don't you go back to bed? No sense in both of us losing sleep."

"When do you estimate the plane will land, if it lands tonight?" she asked.

"The man or men will need time to get up to the mesa and set out the flares. Around midnight, I guess."

"It must be almost that now. I'll wait."

They stood in silence. The darkness was filled with the usual night sounds. Though all her senses were alert, she heard nothing out of the ordinary, until the sound of a distant engine penetrated the night.

"There! See it?" Jane asked, belatedly realizing that she was whispering.

Santiago glanced at his watch. "Right on time. Let's see how long it takes them to transact their business."

Jane remained quietly by his side for several minutes. Finally she couldn't keep still any longer. "I can't believe this . . . whatever it is, is happening on my ranch! I had so hoped that we were wrong!"

Santiago laid a hand consolingly on her shoulder. "Don't upset yourself. If smuggling is going on, the smugglers will be caught."

Before she could ask him just how that was going to happen and who would catch them, they heard the plane again.

"Fourteen minutes. They're well organized and efficient," Santiago said, reluctant admiration in his voice.

"I'd like to know what it is they're so efficient about."

"Unloading or loading the plane."

"Drugs?"

"Maybe, but it could also be arms or contraband liquor."

Jane gasped. "This gets worse and worse."

Her voice was filled with such despair that Santiago placed his arms around Jane and drew her close. Softly he whispered some words in Spanish—words of comfort, words he used to soothe Marisa. When he felt Jane's hands on the bare skin of his back, desire coursed through him like a searing bolt, and the words changed to endearments, words a man used to woo a woman.

He felt the heat of her body. Shocked, he realized that only the wall of a thin cotton gown separated them. Jane shivered, and that small, telling response of her body brought him to his senses. Gritting his teeth, he stepped back.

"It is getting late," he said. "We should get some sleep."

"You're right." Her voice sounded soft and breathy.

Santiago watched her pick up the shotgun she had leaned against the wall and walk into the house. He stayed outside a few minutes longer, letting the night air cool him, wondering if he had been the biggest fool on earth for having let her go.

On Saturday, Jane cleaned house and did laundry. While she kept busy, she couldn't prevent her thoughts from straying to that long, comforting embrace. Not just comforting. A friend's embrace was comforting. Santiago's embrace had been a lot more powerful than that.

His strong arms had pressed her against his bare chest. Her hands, splayed over the smooth expanse of his back, had moved whisper soft over the bands of muscles, delighting in the feel of them. She had leaned her face against his shoulder, her lips touching his skin. She might have pressed a butterfly kiss onto that smooth, warm skin. Remembering, Jane felt hot color flood her face.

How could she have acted like that? She, who had prided herself on her independence, on her self-sufficiency? She had come so close to throwing herself at him. Only the fact that he was honorable, or didn't find her attractive, had sent them to their separate beds. If she wasn't careful, she would give new meaning to the words *lonely widow.*

Never again. From now on she would be doubly watchful. Not so much as a casual touch, she vowed. Then she sighed. Even as she promised that, she knew how hard it was going to be to remain cool and distant. When Santiago was out on the range somewhere, it was easy to vow all sorts of virtuous things. Put him anywhere near her, though, and all the dangerous, sensuous feelings she'd thought dead and forgotten erupted and clamored to be set free. Part of her was afraid of those wild feelings. Part of her rejoiced in them.

"Woman, you're an emotional volcano," she muttered. She picked up the laundry basket and went outside.

While she concentrated on hanging the wash on the clothesline, her gaze kept straying to the mesa. What had that plane delivered or picked up? All day her stomach churned in apprehension, so when Deputy Wilson pulled up in his cruiser, her heart jumped all the way into her throat. Had he found out about the drugs or arms being transported across her land?

"Hey, Jane," Wilson said.

He kept his reflector sunglasses on, but Jane could tell he was giving her the once-over. "Hi, Bud. What can I do for you?"

"The question should be, what can I do for you," he said with a smirk.

"And what's that?" Jane hung up the last towel. She picked up the laundry basket, wedged it against her hips, and waited for his reply.

"Heard you might have some trespassers on your mesa. Thought I'd ride up there and take a look."

"Not today."

"And why not today?"

"I've got a bunch of guests camping up there."

"And you don't want to lose your income from those greenhorns," he said with a slightly superior tone.

His tone irritated her, and the term *greenhorn* struck her as theatrical, but she didn't challenge him on either. "They're not just *my* paying customers. They buy gas and groceries in town

and hire local help, all of which brings in revenue for the town."
And helped pay his salary.

"You have a point there," Wilson said, hitching up his pants.
"I'll come back some other time." He turned toward the mesa
and stopped abruptly. "Who's that?" he demanded, nodding
toward Santiago, who was repairing the corral gate.

"My hired hand, Santiago."

Wilson whipped off his sunglasses and glowered at Jane.
"You hired one of *them?*" he asked, his face red with anger.
"You hired a beaner? Your husband's turning over in his grave."

Jane was so shocked, she could only stare at Wilson.

"Roy was a red-blooded American. A true Texan. A rodeo
champion. A local hero. How could you hire one of *them* to
work on his ranch?" Wilson demanded.

She counted to eight before she allowed herself to speak.
"First of all, I don't remember Roy's being a bigot. Second,
the ranch never belonged to him but to my family. Third, I can
hire anyone I want. All I ask is that they be hardworking and
honest. And fourth, it's none of your business whom I hire."

"Hell, yes, it is. I'm an official deputy, hired and sworn to
uphold the law and to keep the illegals out, hired—"

"Nobody here's illegal or has broken any laws," Jane said
staunchly, hoping to high heaven her claim was right. "Bud,
we're no longer in grade school. You can't bully me now. Unless
you have a warrant of some kind, I suggest you get off my land.
Now." Jane watched him struggle to control his temper.

"I'll be back. You can count on that, and that wetback's
papers better be in order." With a last sneering look in Santiago's direction, Wilson got into his cruiser and drove off.

Jane's knees felt weak. She made it to the porch, where she
sat down heavily.

Santiago joined her, his expression serious. "What's wrong?"

Jane shook her head. "Bud Wilson was one of those kids
who bullied from kindergarten on. Now he's an adult bully,
and, thanks to his job, he has the law's sanction to continue to
ride roughshod over people. Still, I should have handled him
better. Blast."

"He's a minor tyrant. What can he do to you?"

"I'm not worried about me. Are you sure your papers are in order?"

"I'm sure. Why?"

"Because Wilson will make it his business to check."

"Let him."

Santiago's answer was so supremely confident that Jane felt a little ashamed for even having asked about the papers. He was right, though. It was a waste of energy to worry about Wilson. "I'd better go in and start supper. Such as it is."

"What's wrong?" Santiago asked softly.

"Nothing. Everything. I guess I'm a little down." She shrugged. "I get so tired of fixing the same things: beef and canned vegetables. Until two years ago I put in a large garden behind the house. We had fresh vegetables from spring till fall. And flowers. Such pretty flowers."

Jane looked so wistful that Santiago had to restrain himself from putting his arms around her.

"This year I didn't even bother to put in a single radish. I can't afford to water a garden. I'm praying as it is that the wells won't run dry."

"The drought will end. It always does."

Jane was no longer sure she believed that.

Returning from church on Sunday, Jane stopped at her neighbors' place. While she waited in her truck for someone to come outside, she looked around. A new blue pickup caught her eye. Jane felt a pang of envy. Both her trucks had logged nearly two hundred thousand miles. She had no idea when, if ever, she could afford to replace them with anything other than a used vehicle with fewer miles on it.

Penny Long stepped out onto the porch, drying her hands on a dish towel. "Come on in, Jane."

"Nice truck," Jane said, joining Penny on the porch.

Penny shrugged. "Tom's pride and joy. Want to stay for dinner? It's almost ready."

"Thanks, but I have to get back to the ranch. I was wondering if Christie could babysit for a few hours this afternoon."

"I'm sure she can. When do you want her?"

"Around two. I'll come back to get her."

"No need. We're letting her drive the old pickup."

"Great. Thanks."

Driving home, Jane wondered how her neighbors could afford a new truck, especially since they hadn't traded in the old one. Maybe they'd taken a loan against their land, as she had done when she'd assumed ownership of the ranch. Jane prayed that her trucks wouldn't break down—at least not until she'd paid off the existing loan.

"They're late," Jane said, squinting into the sunlit afternoon landscape. "I wonder what went wrong."

"Maybe they got a late start. Lingered over breakfast," Santiago said, standing beside Jane. He placed one booted foot on the lowest rail of the corral. "They might have had vehicle problems. Or trouble with the horses."

Jane shook her head. "That's unlikely. They have experienced wranglers with them who are also pretty good mechanics. Of course, they might have partied extra hard last night."

"Hangovers?"

Jane nodded. "And from what Leanne let drop, some of Susan's guests are not above using recreational drugs. I'm so thankful I don't have Leanne's job." They leaned in silence against the corral until a good-sized dust cloud appeared above the ridge.

"That's got to be them," Santiago said.

Jane turned around, looking for the babysitter, who was on the porch, reading to Marisa. The sight made her smile.

"I'll put the other horses into the second corral. That way we can just drive Susan's into this one," she said to Santiago before she hurried off.

The next few minutes were all dusty confusion, with horses being unloaded and turned loose in the corral, guests getting out of their vehicles to stretch, to demand something to drink, to make calls on their cell phones.

Something wasn't quite right, but Jane couldn't put her finger on what it was. She caught up with Leanne, who looked even more frazzled than usual.

"What's going on?" Jane asked.

"What do you mean?"

"You're late, and you're even letting Byron handle the horses. You don't usually let him near them."

Leanne wiped the back of one arm over her forehead. "Well, I may as well tell you. A couple of the horses got loose and took off. Heaven only knows where they are. I sent two of the wranglers after them in their trucks, but I doubt they'll catch them. Neither of them could track his own footprints in fresh mud at high noon."

"Where did they get loose?"

"On the mesa. Something spooked them."

"Which two horses?" Jane asked.

"The roan. And Goldie, Susan's favorite. She isn't any too pleased with me right now."

The palomino was a valuable horse. Jane made a fast decision. "Don't worry. I'll look for them. Tell Susan. And Santiago." Without waiting for an answer, Jane ran to the second corral, saddled Nifty, and rode out.

The horses had probably taken the main trail down from the mesa. Where they'd gone from there was hard to say, except Jane strongly suspected that they would eventually find their way back to the ranch. She was riding out to mollify Susan.

She stopped periodically to scan the ground, cutting for signs. She never did sight the horses, but a couple of hours later she caught a glimpse of two trucks. Squinting through the dust, she thought they looked like the ones in Susan's caravan. Jane yelled and waved. The drivers must have seen her before an outcropping of rock came between them. Why hadn't they stopped?

A second later, a high-pitched whine startled her. Something hit the dirt to the left of her. It took a dumbfounded moment before Jane realized that someone was shooting at her. Leaning low over Nifty, she urged the mare behind the nearest boulder. She dismounted and stroked Nifty's neck to calm the mare.

What was the matter with those men? Hadn't they recognized her? Jane was about to shout out to them when several bullets hit the ground near her.

Automatically Jane reached for the scabbard before she realized she'd ridden off without the rifle she normally kept there. *Damn.* They had her pinned down. Her heart raced. Her palms sweated.

"Think," she admonished herself. Her best chance to get away was under cover of darkness. Glancing at the sky, she realized that dusk was several hours away. Scratch that plan. She couldn't stay where she was, because as soon as they realized she wasn't shooting back, they'd probably come after her. Confused, she wondered why they were firing at her. Not that it mattered just then. She had to get out of there.

Leading Nifty, she started through the rough terrain of the rocks. It was hard going, but trucks couldn't follow her. Still, there were some open spots where a bullet could catch her. She didn't like the odds, but what other choice did she have? She licked her dry lips.

"Come on, girl," she urged Nifty. They sprinted across the open ground. They reached the next rocks without being hit, but Nifty was getting spooked. With a determined jerk on the reins, Nifty freed herself and took off. A round of bullets followed the horse.

"Bastards!" Jane yelled, and she shook her fist at the men. Thank heaven it was hard to hit a moving target, even one as large as Nifty. Her mare got away. She uttered a triumphant "Yes!" before the seriousness of her situation sobered her.

She was now on foot. The good thing was that Nifty would run straight home. Santiago would realize something was wrong. She was certain he would come after her. All she had to do was survive until then.

Jane listened intently. Where were the men? How close were they? Had they left their trucks to pursue her? She couldn't stay where she was. She dropped low to the ground. In a crawl she worked her way toward home, yard by rocky yard.

The men continued to shoot, and some of the shots came close, but it was obvious that they were firing randomly. What was bad was that in this crawling mode she couldn't cover much ground. Worse, her canteen was in the saddlebag, riding with Nifty toward the ranch. And even though it was late afternoon, the earth beneath her felt as if it was heated by a furnace. Jane tied her bandana around her forehead to keep the sweat from blinding her.

Suddenly a bullet pinged off the rock behind her. How was that possible? With horror Jane realized that it was a ricochet. She had to put more distance between herself and the shooters. With a determined effort, she sprinted until she was breathless, and then she crawled again. Through the wild beating of her heart and her labored breaths, she heard a new sound: a rifle being fired from somewhere in front of her. And, miraculously, the bullets weren't aimed at her.

Someone was helping her. Santiago? No, Nifty couldn't have reached the ranch that quickly. Whoever it was fired a barrage of bullets at the men.

She spied movement to her right. *Santiago!* Firing rapidly, he sprinted from one rock cover to the next. He reached her just before bullets sprayed the area he had just vacated.

"Are you all right?" he asked, shoving a new clip into his pistol.

"Yes. Am I glad to see you."

"Ever shot one of these?" he asked.

"A pistol? Yes, but I'm a better shot with a rifle."

Santiago handed Jane the rifle and a box of ammunition. "On three, we'll both fire. They're behind the rocks at one o'clock. That's a little to the right," he added. "Okay?"

Jane nodded. On his command they both fired. They repeated this maneuver twice more. As they reloaded their weapons, they heard the trucks start and drive off.

"They're leaving," Jane said, her voice disbelieving. "Why? Not that I'm complaining, but they had us pinned down."

"They are more interested in getting out of here. Besides, we were evenly matched in firepower. They couldn't have rushed us."

"So they're getting away."

"Only this time."

She glanced at Santiago. His face was like a mask, and the absence of any emotion from his tone made the implied threat doubly menacing. Jane was glad he was on her side.

"Nifty couldn't have made it back to the ranch yet. How did you get here so fast?"

"I left as soon as the caravan drove off. I was tempted to leave the moment Leanne told me you rode out—"

"You were right to stay until they left," Jane assured him. "But I'm awfully glad you came when you did." She placed a hand on his arm and squeezed it gently, gratefully.

"When I heard the gunfire, my heart nearly stopped. I knew you hadn't taken a rifle with you. Promise that from now on, you'll never leave the ranch without one."

His eyes, his voice, so emotionless only seconds before, were now filled with tender concern for her. Jane felt her throat grow tight. All she could do was nod.

Santiago took her hands in his. When she heard his indrawn breath, she looked at his face, which had grown pale. Following his gaze to see what made him mutter some terse words in Spanish, she saw that her hands and arms were scratched and bloodied.

"Those are only superficial scratches from crawling over the rocks. I didn't even notice them until now."

"Whoever did this will pay."

The intensity of the simple words made her shiver. He raised her hands to his lips to kiss each bruise. Jane understood for the first time why a man's touch might make a woman feel as if the earth trembled.

Chapter Four

Santiago still held her hands in his. They looked at each other for a long moment. It seemed to Jane that there were hundreds of things she wanted to say, needed to say, and yet she couldn't utter a single one.

She felt herself sway toward him, but surely that was only an emotional illusion. They had just shared moments of grave danger, had felt the breath of death, so it was no wonder that every subsequent emotion, every sensation, seemed heightened and intensified. But the emotional danger they faced now was every bit as serious as the physical danger they had faced from the bullets minutes earlier. Jane willed her breathing to slow down.

"You think the shooters might come back?" she asked.

"No. Let's look around."

They examined the area where the men had parked the trucks. Santiago pocketed several spent shells before he squatted down to study the tire marks.

Jane joined him. She used the nail of one index finger to measure the indentation the tires had made. "This isn't an accurate measurement, but it seems to me that some of these markings are deeper than the others."

"They are. The trucks are carrying more weight going down than they did coming up the mesa."

"I'd hoped our suspicions would be proven wrong."

"Because this was Susan Baldwin's group?"

"No, because I'd hoped that nothing illegal was going on. But that wasn't a realistic hope, was it?"

"I'm afraid not."

"What I don't understand is why those men opened fire on me. I was only going to ask them if they'd seen the horses."

"Maybe they didn't recognize you and didn't want to be questioned. Or, more likely, they simply panicked. If caught"—Santiago paused to correct himself—"*when* caught, they'll spend a long time in prison."

"What do you think was on the trucks? Drugs or arms?"

"If I had to guess, I'd say drugs, simply because along the border the drug business is bigger than the arms trade. The trucks were probably loaded with bales of marijuana."

"Bales? Like bales of hay?"

"Marijuana is a plant. Also known as *grass,* remember?"

"I know, but bales of it?"

"The bales aren't that big. Probably weigh about forty pounds. So, if the drug lords can't find any other transportation, they hire men who can carry that much across the border on their backs."

Jane stared at him as if she couldn't believe what she was hearing. Finally she repeated, "On their backs. Wrapped in what? I'm trying to envision this whole nightmarish scenario."

"Usually wrapped in plastic and secured with duct tape and then put into a burlap sack that's worn like a backpack."

Jane sat heavily on the ground, drew her knees to her chest, and wound her arms around them.

Santiago didn't interrupt her thoughts, suspecting that she was trying to come to some decision.

Quietly she said, "I respect people's privacy because I value my own, but the time has come when I have to ask you some questions."

"I thought you might." He sat on the ground beside her.

"You know a lot about drugs and arms smuggling. You own night-vision goggles, a fancy handgun—"

"It's a Glock. Not fancy—"

"I didn't mean fancy in that way. More that it's uncommon. At least in this part of the country. Anyway, you know things, have things, that ordinary people don't. Who are you?" Jane looked into his eyes. He didn't blink, didn't look away. He seemed to be debating with himself. She waited.

"I know I owe you an explanation, but I can't go into details. Please understand that."

She regarded him skeptically but finally inclined her head. "All right. Tell me what you can."

"There was a time when I worked for your government. Undercover. That's why I know about smuggling."

Jane stared at him. "Are you still undercover?"

"With a baby as part of my cover? Risking her life? No, Jane, I'm not."

"The government just let you quit?"

"I was on medical leave." Without volition, his right hand touched the scar on his forehead. "Then I asked for a leave of absence to . . . to take care of some things."

"You were hurt while working for the government?"

"Yes." Santiago knew Jane wanted details, details he couldn't give her. "Jane, believe me when I say that now I *am* a cowboy, a ranch hand. I work for you. What's the saying? 'What you see is what you get'?"

Jane doubted that but said nothing, thinking about what he'd told her.

"You don't believe me?" Santiago finally asked.

"I don't think you out-and-out lied, but I suspect you've left out big chunks of the truth." She rose. "We'd better head back. It'll be dark soon. You didn't by chance meet Nifty on the way up here, did you?"

"No. We'll have to double up on my horse."

With Jane riding behind him, her arms wrapped lightly around his waist, Santiago found it hard to concentrate, to recall every word he'd said to her.

He had known she would start asking questions. How could she not? She was intelligent and observant. She reminded him of the women in his family. Had he told Jane too much? He hoped not, for the last thing he wanted was to endanger her life. She was already in danger from those trigger-happy fools.

He also knew that she didn't entirely believe him. Again, why should she? His story had holes in it big enough to drive a herd of cattle through. He couldn't fill in those gaps. At least not yet.

What an incredible lady she was. Most women would demand details, proof, assurances, and heaven only knew what else. But not Jane. She accepted him on faith. He felt humbled by her trust, by the generosity of her spirit. And he was totally turned on by her. He could almost feel the taste of her lips on his.

Jane had much to think about as she went about her chores the next day. Santiago hadn't told her a lot, and what he had told her sounded almost fantastical. Secret government work? Undercover agent? Weren't the odds far greater that he was a drug runner rather than an undercover agent? Undoubtedly, and yet . . .

Why was she hesitant to believe him to be a smuggler? Because she was attracted to him? Liked him? Because of Marisa? Probably for all those reasons. And because of something else. She couldn't pinpoint the quality in Santiago that made her place him on the side of the angels, but she sensed some bone-deep goodness in him, some basic honor in his character that led her to believe him, to trust him.

What if she was wrong? *No.* Santiago loved Marisa, and he cared for a damaged bird. Mentally Jane continued to line up pluses and minuses for Santiago until her head was spinning.

She had to have some answers, answers she could trust. It was time for a long talk with Father Anselmo.

"Baby girl, you and I are going for a drive," she said to little Marisa.

"Baby girl, baby girl," Paco said.

"I wish you wouldn't repeat everything. It's annoying."

"Baby girl, baby girl."

Jane decided it was best to ignore Paco. She lifted Marisa from the playpen, grabbed her purse, and headed for the door. There she stopped. Santiago might get back to the house before she returned from town. Hastily, she wrote him a note and placed it on the kitchen table.

Sitting at Father Anselmo's dining room table, Jane tried to hide her impatience. She pleated the linen napkin on her lap. She tapped her foot. She hoped that the table hid these nervous reactions from Father Anselmo. She had finished her coffee in record time, but the good padre let his cool while he entertained Marisa with his keys. When his housekeeper came back to see if they needed anything else, he asked her to take care of the baby while he talked with Jane.

"I appreciate your letting me hold Marisa. I know you are anxious to talk to me about whatever it is that's bothering you," he said with a twinkle in his eye.

"I can never fool you, can I?" She took a deep breath and simply blurted it out. "What's bothering me is Santiago."

"Why? What happened? Tell me everything."

Jane did. When she finished, she looked straight at Father Anselmo and said, "Please answer one question. Is he an ex-government agent?" She watched Father Anselmo blink. For once he seemed to be at a loss for words. The sip of coffee he took was clearly a delaying tactic.

"What makes you think Santiago is an ex-agent?"

"He told me he was."

"I'm surprised. I was sure he wanted to keep that under wraps."

Jane swallowed before she asked, her voice barely above a whisper, "You mean it's true?"

"Yes."

Jane felt a wave of pure joy surge through her. Santiago was not a drug runner. He *was* one of the good guys. Just to make sure, she asked, "How do you know that? Do you have proof?"

"Yes. Jane, I can't reveal any more. You have to ask him if you want details."

Jane groaned. "You two share the same theme song: 'I can't tell you any more,'" she said, her voice coming as close to being critical of Father Anselmo as it had ever come.

"I'm sorry. I know this must be somewhat frustrating—"

"*Somewhat? Try totally* frustrating." Jane studied Father Anselmo as if she were seeing him for the first time.

"What is it you're wondering about?"

"I'm surprised at you, Father. You've never meddled with politics or the government. Well, you occasionally took on social services and welfare on behalf of your parishioners, but that was it. Now you're involved with covert undercover operations and heaven only knows what else."

Father Anselmo made a dismissing gesture.

"Seriously, I'm worried. You remember the liberation theology priests? They ran into big trouble. Some were arrested, tortured, and—"

"Jane, that happened in Latin America. This is the United States. Thanks for worrying, but I'm in no danger."

The housekeeper knocked on the door to tell Father Anselmo that he had a phone call.

"I have a parcel I want you to take to Santiago." He removed a nine-by-twelve-inch package from the sideboard and held it out to Jane.

She hesitated a beat before she accepted it. "I suppose if I asked what was in this package or who it was from, you'd say that you couldn't tell me." Jane watched a smile light up the padre's face, a smile that took years off his careworn features.

"No, I'd say that I had no idea what's in the package. And that's the truth. Go in peace, Jane."

After she'd strapped the baby into the car seat, Jane examined the package. She managed to decipher part of the postmark. It had been mailed in Maryland. Whom did Santiago know in Maryland? When she remembered that Maryland bordered Washington, D.C., a shiver rippled along her spine.

Weren't all those government agencies usually referred to only by their initials located in and around the nation's capital? What if they wanted Santiago to work for them again? Take him away? Endanger his life? She shivered again.

For an instant Jane thought of all the lonely places on the way home where she could lose this package, but even as she entertained the tempting thought, she knew she would take it to Santiago.

He was late. Studying the trail leading to the mesa and committing its features to memory had taken longer than Santiago had anticipated. If he had quit mending the fence sooner, he wouldn't have been late, but he felt he owed Jane a decent day's work. After all, he was in her employ now, not the government's.

"I'm sorry I'm late," he said as soon as he entered the kitchen. "I hope you ate and didn't wait for me." Only then he noticed that the table was set for two. "You did wait." That considerate gesture pleased him enormously.

"You're not that late," Jane said. She took a bowl from the oven, where she'd kept the food warm. She uncovered it and frowned. "The mashed potatoes are probably past their prime."

"I'm sure they're still good. Give me five minutes to clean up. Is Marisa asleep?"

Jane nodded. "Her tooth came through. She stopped fussing."

Santiago checked on Marisa. She was lying on her side, her hand resting on the rattle she liked to bang against the sides of the crib. As always when he looked at her, he thought of his sister and his mother, both dead before their time. Marisa was the only link to them he had left. He bent down and pressed a soft kiss onto the baby's cheek.

Unobtrusively, Jane watched Santiago eat. Though eight work-filled hours had passed since lunch and he had to be ravenously hungry, he ate slowly, seemingly appreciating the pot roast she had cooked. When he leaned forward to pick up his water glass, the overhead light made his hair shimmer blue-black. Raven black. Why did she always associate nature images with Santiago? The eyes of a wolf. The silent, graceful movements of a panther. The color of a raven. Maybe because she felt a deep kinship to nature and generally liked animals better than people?

"What are you thinking?" he asked.

Caught. Flustered, Jane shrugged. Improvising, she said, "That it's a pleasure to cook for a man who enjoys food."

"Why wouldn't I? You're a good cook."

"But not fancy."

"Fancy doesn't automatically mean good. I've been served some so-called fancy meals that were barely edible, but everything you've fixed for me has been excellent."

Jane knew that the pleasure his compliment gave her tinged her face with warm color. Quickly and a little wistfully, she said, "I'll bet, though, that those fancy meals were served on white tablecloths with fine china and silver. There was probably a fancy flower arrangement on the table and soft candlelight that made the elegantly dressed women look even more lovely."

She touched the rim of her plate, which had a tiny chip in it. She'd been meaning to get her crockery replaced, but the money always went to more urgently needed things, such as a new water pump or medicine for the calves or new tires for the trucks.

"Jane," Santiago said softly, "those things don't matter. Yes, I've eaten at beautifully set tables. I've also eaten cold beans straight out of a can in the company of men who hadn't washed in so long that even the mosquitoes wouldn't come near them." When she didn't say anything, he added, "As for elegantly dressed women . . . frankly, I'm old enough to look beyond the trappings of clothes and makeup and jewelry."

Makeup and jewelry? She wasn't wearing either. And her jeans and faded T-shirt, though clean and ironed, wouldn't win any fashion awards. The things he had seen and done, the circles he had moved in, were light-years from her world. Did they have *anything* in common? She chastised herself for even wondering about that. Though they shared a house, and a disturbingly strong physical attraction simmered between them, theirs was strictly a working relationship.

"Have you seen any of Jeanne Moreau's movies?" Santiago asked.

Jane shook her head. "Who's she?"

"A French actress who was popular some years ago."

Jane slanted him an ironic look. "French films don't make it often to this part of the country. Why do you ask?"

"Because you look like her."

Jane stopped eating. "Really," she said. It wasn't a question but a one-word statement of disbelief.

"Really," he repeated. "She's beautiful, and so are you."

Jane put her fork down. She searched his face for clues.

"What are you wondering about?"

"Why you'd say something like that to me."

"Try 'because it's the truth.'" From her expression he realized that she didn't believe him. Santiago leaned forward. "Let me try to explain."

Looking into her dark eyes that regarded him with quiet watchfulness, he said, "There are probably as many different kinds of beauty as there are women. There's the fresh loveliness of a young girl. The hollow-cheeked beauty of a model. The glamorous appeal of a film star, and so on. Then there's the serene, severe, silent beauty of a woman like you."

Jane blinked. "'Serene, severe, and silent'?" she asked, her voice reflecting that she didn't think much of this description.

"Yes. The beauty of a woman who has survived some severe blows, such as the loss of her husband, far too soon. Blows that would have brought a weaker woman to her knees. Hers is the deepest, finest kind of beauty."

"Serene, severe, and silent," Jane repeated again, but this time thoughtfully.

Santiago smiled ruefully. "Too much alliteration." He shook his head. "When I was young and before my life took off in a totally different direction, I thought about becoming a writer," he confessed. "It's too late now."

"Why? Seems to me you've gathered a lot of experience in recent years that you could use in your writing."

"There's the matter of time. Writing takes time."

"We're not always so busy. During the winter it's downright slow around here." What had possessed her to say that? She had no idea what Santiago's plans were, and here she'd said something that sounded as if she expected him to stick around. Quickly she said, "For a woman described as being silent, I seem to do a lot of talking." She got up and started to clear the table.

"Silence is good. It's peaceful. Quiet, a good meal, and the company of a woman with a soft, sexy voice and a restful nature is something a man appreciates after a hard day's work."

"A 'restful nature'? I'm not sure I like that description. Makes me sound boring."

"Restful in the sense that you don't complain, nag, argue, or chatter. A lot of people feel compelled to fill silence with chit-chat. You don't. I like that about you."

Santiago carried his plate to the sink. For a moment he laid a hand on Jane's shoulder. "Hasn't anyone told you how pleasing your quietness is?"

"Only my grandfather. He always said he couldn't abide chatty, gossipy women."

"Not your husband?"

Santiago stood so close that their bodies were almost touching. Jane felt the warmth of his hand through the cotton of her shirt. She found it difficult to think straight. She wasn't sure her tongue wasn't lamed. She had to pull herself together.

"Is it difficult for you to speak of your husband?"

"No, it isn't that. I'm not sure what my husband thought. He liked to talk and be around a lot of people." *Especially women.* Jane turned the faucet on full force, effectively ending their conversation.

"I'll go check on the horses one more time." Santiago briefly touched her hair, reveling in its silky texture. Then he left quickly.

Jane took a deep breath and expelled it. She leaned against the sink. Actually, Roy had accused her of being moody. He had mistaken her quietness for moodiness. Santiago hadn't made that mistake. Although he'd known her only a short time, he seemed to understand her in ways her husband never had. That pleased her—until she recognized the danger it represented.

It was foolish and dangerous to allow herself to grow too fond of this man about whom she knew so little. This man who couldn't or wouldn't reveal himself. What she had hoped for most in her marriage and hadn't received was true emotional intimacy. What were the chances of such closeness with Santiago? Zero.

Jane gritted her teeth and concentrated on scrubbing the dishes in the sink.

The next day's mail brought an unpleasant surprise. A letter from the bank was signed by a vice president Jane had never met. She hadn't even known that the small, independent bank had a vice president.

"You seem worried," Santiago said, seated at the table. He had picked up the mail from their mailbox by the highway on his way to the house for lunch.

Jane set a filled plate in front of him, her eyes still on the letter.

"Trouble?" he asked.

"I don't know. Mr. Alexander, the bank president, always renewed my loan automatically. Now I get a letter from a vice president I've never heard of, telling me the loan is due in three weeks. I don't understand." She frowned at the letter.

"What would happen if the loan isn't—"

"Don't even think that." Jane felt the need to steady herself by holding on to the back of the nearest chair. "I'd better phone this vice president and find out what's going on."

Chapter Five

"Father Anselmo. Good to see you," Santiago said, coming out of the barn. He shook the priest's outstretched hand. "I didn't expect you to come to the ranch."

"I have another package for you. I didn't know how important it was, so I brought it." He smiled a little guiltily. "The truth is, I wanted to know how you all were doing."

"We're fine, Father." Santiago accepted the padded envelope and extracted a note from it. He felt the priest watching him as he read it.

"Good news?" Father Anselmo asked.

"*I* think so."

Picking up on the emphasized pronoun, the priest asked, "But *I* might not think so? Which leads me to assume that you've received official backing from Washington."

"Not exactly," Santiago said.

"What does that mean?"

"It means that I can get a little help on the sly, but officially I don't exist. If something goes wrong, the leader of the Omega Group will disavow all knowledge of me and claim that he thought I was dead. As far as the official records go, I'm still listed as being dead."

"If everything goes according to plan, then what?"

"Then Omega will take the credit for his arrest or his death, and if I want to, I can rejoin."

"Will you?"

Santiago hesitated. "I don't know."

"Your answer seems to surprise you."

"It does," Santiago admitted. "There was a time when I

53

wouldn't have hesitated, when *not* working for the Omega Group would have been unthinkable. Now . . ." Santiago shrugged. Looking at the padre, who was smiling, he added, "My hesitation appears to please you, Father."

"It does. It does indeed. There are any number of things you can do with your life that do not involve violence. Productive things. Things beneficial to others. Even creative things." Father Anselmo paused for a moment. Quietly he added, "Remember that those who live by the sword . . ." His voice trailed off.

"Die by it. I know the quotation," Santiago said drily. "But wrongs have to be put right—for Corazon, for Marisa, and for many others."

"Let the law do it."

Santiago shook his head, his expression unyieldingly stubborn. "Right now the law cannot touch the guilty, so it's up to me to see that justice is done."

"Are you sure it's justice and not vengeance you want?"

For a moment Santiago was startled. Then quickly and firmly he said, "I am sure, but you don't look convinced."

"Sometimes we lie to ourselves. Sometimes it's hard to identify our true motives and even harder to admit what they are. Examine your heart carefully," the priest exhorted.

"I will."

Father Anselmo looked into Santiago's eyes for a long beat before he nodded. Glancing around, he asked, "Where's Jane?"

"She drove into town to talk to the vice president of the bank."

"She probably doesn't know that the bank's been sold. We're now but one branch of a state-wide banking system."

"I'm sure she didn't know," Santiago said, his tone worried. "I hope that won't cause her a major problem."

"I do too. Tell her I stopped by."

Santiago touched the priest's arm to stop him from leaving. "Father, may I ask you a couple of questions?"

"Of course. Ask."

"Did you know Jane's husband?"

"I did."

Pretending a casualness he didn't feel, Santiago asked, "What was he like? Jane doesn't say much about him." Santiago half expected the padre to be surprised by the question and possibly demand to know why Santiago wanted this information, but Father Anselmo took the question in stride.

"Roy was one of those lucky people on whom life seemed to smile. He was good-looking, personable, easygoing, and generous to a fault. People liked Roy. Both men and women. When he wanted to, he could charm the birds out of a tree."

Santiago waited. Finally he said, "I have the impression that there's a 'but' hovering in the air."

Father Anselmo shrugged, his expression sheepish. "There is. For all his good qualities, Roy was also . . . let me just say that he was the wrong man for Jane. I couldn't believe it when she told me that she had married him. I've known her all her life, and impulsiveness is not one of Jane's character traits."

He sighed before he continued. "Of course, she was young. Just fresh out of college when she met him. He swept her off her feet, and six weeks later they were married. The old adage 'marry in haste' comes to mind." He shrugged. "Maybe the marriage would have survived, but I rather doubt it. Impulse marriages rarely do."

When Father Anselmo didn't elaborate, Santiago couldn't keep himself from pushing for more information. "Why was he the wrong man for Jane?"

"Because he and Jane had diametrically opposed life expectations. She wanted a home, a couple of kids, and a settled, peaceful existence with a faithful husband. Roy wasn't faithful, and I suspect Jane knew that. He was not a domestic man. He craved the danger, the excitement, and the violence of the rodeo." Father Anselmo cast a sidelong glance at Santiago. "In that craving you're like him."

Santiago raised a doubting eyebrow. "It may look as if I

crave excitement, but I don't. Not by nature. I was thrown into a life of violence. I had no choice then."

"But now you have options."

"Maybe. After justice is meted out."

Father Anselmo shook his head sorrowfully. "That's what makes a life of violence so dangerous. It is addictive. Be careful, my son, that you don't lose your way."

Santiago watched the priest drive away. Much of what the good padre had said was true. Some men embraced violence as a way of life until violence claimed them in the final embrace of a brutal death. Was he in danger of becoming like that? He didn't think so. He fervently hoped not.

All he wanted to do was settle the score. After that, he and Jane . . . He clamped down on that seductive thought. He couldn't be distracted by anyone or anything. Not even by daydreams of a future with the woman who occupied his thoughts much too much.

Jane concentrated on the salad greens she'd brought from town. She knew she would have to talk to Santiago about what had happened at the bank, but she was putting it off as long as possible.

"Marisa likes the high chair you brought her," Santiago said.

"She seems to," Jane said, looking at the baby with a smile. "I bought it at the consignment shop Father Anselmo's housekeeper runs out of the church basement. I also got one of those collapsible strollers, since Marisa is getting too big for her buggy. Both were good buys."

"He was here this morning."

"Father Anselmo? To see you or me?"

"Both of us." Santiago waited. When Jane didn't ask, he added, "He had a package for me."

Alarm slammed through Jane. What was in those packages? Santiago hadn't opened the first package in front of her and hadn't mentioned it, but Jane had a bad feeling about the packages. She swallowed hard. In a small voice she asked, "Does that mean you have to leave?"

"No. I told you, I don't work for the government anymore."

Jane's hold on the head of romaine eased. She noticed she had crushed the outer leaves, which she now discarded. So, the government hadn't asked Santiago to leave. If he left, it would be by his choice. Jane wasn't sure if that would make his leaving harder to take or not.

"What happened at the bank?"

Jane looked over her shoulder at him. She shrugged. "Mr. Alexander had a heart attack. He'll recover, but he had to sell the bank. The new owners are a different breed." Jane poured dressing over the salad and carried it to the table.

"The new vice president, who's probably younger than I am, listened to me. He said he would take my case under advisement." Jane rolled her eyes. "I'm not kidding. He actually said 'under advisement' in this really pompous voice. He'll let me know if they can renew my loan. If not . . ." Her voice faltered and broke off.

"Did he say how soon he'd let you know?"

"Probably by the end of the week. Or the beginning of next." Jane aligned her place mat with the edge of the table. Then she moved her water glass an inch to the right. When she had her agitation under control, she said, "It was all very businesslike. Frosty. Impersonal. I miss Mr. Alexander."

"Maybe this new man will mellow," Santiago said.

"Maybe, but he's not from around here. He'll never understand our ways. Mr. Alexander knew that everything moves in cycles. A drought is followed by rain. A slump in the cattle business is succeeded by a rise in beef prices. We just have to wait things out. And while we wait, we can't pay our loans off. We always do, though, when things get better."

Jane paused in her impassioned speech. She managed a small, apologetic smile. "I'm sorry for the lecture."

"You can lecture me anytime," Santiago said, knowing how worried and upset she was.

She pulled the salad bowl closer. "Let me serve you. I splurged and bought three different kinds of lettuce," she said, her voice bravely defiant. "I intend to enjoy this treat."

And she did, despite her worry over the loan. However, her enjoyment was short-lived. While she cleared the table, she heard a car pull up.

"Now what?" she muttered. She walked to the window to look out.

"Who is it?"

"Deputy Wilson. I must not live right."

Santiago wiped Marisa's mouth with a napkin before he lifted her from the high chair. "I seem to rub the deputy the wrong way," Santiago said. "I'll put Marisa down for her nap."

Jane allowed her eyes to watch Santiago walk down the hall. He moved with a natural gracefulness that was a pleasure to observe. Reluctantly, she went to the front porch and waited for the deputy to approach.

"Hey, Jane."

"Bud. Did you come to take a look at the mesa?"

"Well, I could, I guess," he said without enthusiasm.

"As large as your territory is, I can't believe you felt like taking a ride out here for no reason."

"Well, no."

"Did you come to share your good news?" Jane asked.

"What are you talking about?"

"When I was in town, I ran into Mrs. Gibson."

"That old gossip? What did she tell you?"

"Among other things, she said that you and Missy Shuster are a serious item. That you two are courtin' to beat the band. Congratulations, Bud. Missy is a good woman."

Wilson shifted his weight from one foot to the other. "Well, yeah, but that's not what brings me out here." He squared his shoulders. "I came to talk to your hired hand."

Jane had been afraid of that. So much for trying to distract the deputy with small talk.

"You want to see me, deputy?" Santiago asked, opening the screen door.

Jane noticed the angry red color that suffused Wilson's face when he saw Santiago come out of the house.

"What is the problem?" Santiago asked.

"The problem, *amigo,* is that your visa expires in thirty days. Actually, it's twenty-nine as of today."

"I am aware of that," Santiago said.

Jane marveled at Santiago's cool demeanor. She was spitting mad at the pleasure Wilson obviously felt in bringing this bad news.

"Jane?" Wilson motioned Jane to follow him a few steps from the house. In a low but furious voice he demanded, "What's he doing in your house?"

She stared at him, puzzled.

"Seems to me the likes of him should be confined to the bunkhouse. You're a single woman, and he's a—"

"Stop right there." Barely containing her anger, she said, "Santiago eats in the house, as most hired hands do. Smaller ranches around here can't afford to keep a cook on the payroll, and for the hired hands to fix their own meals takes too long. There's way too much work that needs to be done to waste time. You've lived here all your life. You should know that."

Jane turned sharply and walked back to the porch. She stood beside Santiago, her arms folded across her chest. She had chosen sides.

Wilson took a couple of steps toward the porch. He stared hard at Santiago. Hoisting his gun belt up and letting his hand linger on his weapon, he said, "If you're thinking of applying for an extension to your visa, go ahead. It's only fair to tell you, though, that in all the years I've been a deputy, the INS has granted an extension only once. And that was because of mighty extraordinary circumstances."

Jane asked, "What extraordinary circumstances cause the INS to renew a visa?"

"Death of a close relative. Period."

"That's it?" Jane asked.

"Yup. Unless Santiago here can persuade some gullible U.S. female citizen to marry him." Wilson snickered. Then, raising an index finger for emphasis, he said to Santiago, "Let me warn you. The INS is cracking down on these sham marriages. It's not as easy to fool them as it used to be."

Jane bit her tongue to remain silent.

Wilson touched his hand to his hat in a half-mocking salute. "Remember, twenty-nine days." With that he got into his patrol car and drove off.

Neither Jane nor Santiago said anything until Wilson's car was out of sight.

Finally Jane asked, "Is he right about the twenty-nine days?"

"I am afraid so."

Jane reached for the porch railing and leaned against it. Her heart was racing faster than a stampeding herd. In less than a month she might lose Marisa. And Santiago. That couldn't be! She took two shallow breaths to ease the pressure around her heart. "There has to be something we can do. Can't the people in Washington help you?"

"No. That would . . . No." He shook his head. "I have already applied for an extension. Father Anselmo helped me do that before I came to the ranch. But it wouldn't hurt to send a follow-up letter."

Jane jumped on that. "Yes. Let's do it right now." Hurriedly she led the way into the house. "Grandpa left me his typewriter. It's an old manual Smith-Corona, but it works."

"You want me to write the letter now? There are all those chores—"

"Now, please," Jane said, her voice decisive. "If you do it now, I can get it to the mailbox before the carrier gets there. He'll take it and post it today."

"All right. Where's the typewriter?"

"On the bottom shelf in the pantry."

He returned moments later with the machine and a package of typing paper. He set both on the kitchen table. Santiago trailed his fingers over the keys, his expression thoughtful.

"My father had one just like this," he said quietly. "I used to watch him type his papers on it."

"He was a writer?"

"A university professor. He wrote articles for scientific journals."

"You obviously went to college. What did you study?"

"Law, unfortunately."

"Why 'unfortunately'?"

"Because the legal system of each country is unique to that country. If I had studied math or one of the sciences, I might be able to get a job in those disciplines in this country. That kind of knowledge is universal."

Jane nodded that she understood. This was the first time that Santiago had opened up about his past. Jane fretted over how to approach the subject she was intensely curious about. She couldn't just ask him outright. Casually—at least she hoped it was casual—she asked, "Did you meet your wife while you were in college?"

"No. Paloma was the daughter of family friends. She went to school in Switzerland."

Paloma. What an elegant name. Going to school in Switzerland suggested an expensive private-school education. Jane envisioned Santiago's wife as an elegant, refined, possibly pampered woman—everything Jane wasn't.

"What else would you like to know about Paloma?"

Jane looked at him, surprised. "It doesn't bother you to talk about her, even though you lost her so recently?" She watched Santiago's expression turn bewildered.

"What makes you think my wife died recently?"

"Because of Marisa. She's only—"

"You think Marisa is my daughter?" Santiago stared at Jane. Then he tapped his forehead with the palm of his hand. "Of course. Why wouldn't you? A man comes to your door with a baby. It's only natural to assume the baby is his. I'm sorry. I didn't mean to mislead you."

"My fault as much as yours. I jumped to conclusions." Jane paused, thinking of how to phrase her question tactfully. "You obviously love Marisa. Whose baby is she?"

"My sister's. Marisa is my niece."

"You said her mother was dead. What about her father?"

"My brother-in-law was killed as well. I am all she has. *Pobrecita,*" he murmured.

"She is lucky to have you."

"Thank you."

The smile he lavished on her made Jane's insides quiver. If his smile had the power to do that to her, what would a heated kissing session lead to? *Don't even go there,* she told herself. She had to focus on her chance to ask Santiago more questions.

"Were you married long before you became a widower?"

"Just over three years."

Bemused, she said, "I was married just a little under three years." A short marriage and widowhood was something they had in common.

"Father Anselmo mentioned that you married young."

"You discussed me with the padre?" Jane asked.

"Briefly. I wondered about your husband just as you wondered about my wife."

"Point taken. Tell me about Paloma."

"There's not much to tell. She was beautiful. And I was too young not to be taken in by her beauty. My mother tried to tell me that Paloma was willful and demanding, but I didn't listen. She was the only child of wealthy parents who spoiled her shamelessly."

So, Paloma had been a high-maintenance woman, and Santiago, she suspected, wasn't a man who had much patience with that kind of female. For reasons she didn't want to examine too closely, that pleased Jane. "You said you were both young."

"Too young. I wonder if the marriage would have lasted. I didn't get a chance to find out. Coming home from a party, she ran her car off the road and was killed."

Giving in to impulse, Jane reached out and took his hand in hers. She pressed it. "I know what it's like to receive that kind of news and deal with the shock and the loss."

Santiago nodded. He raised her hand to his lips and kissed it.

Jane's heart skipped a beat. For an instant she wanted to throw her arms around his neck. Then her saner self took control. Removing her hand from his, she took a step back.

"If you don't write that letter now, I'll miss the mailman. Every day counts."

"You're right. It does." Santiago rolled a sheet of paper into the machine and started to type.

The week passed slowly. Every day Jane rushed to the mailbox to look for a letter from the bank, and every day she found nothing except some junk mail and a few bills. Friday was no exception.

"I suppose no news is good news," she said to the baby, who gurgled and blew bubbles. Jane kissed Marisa's satin-soft cheek. "You sure love to ride in this truck, don't you, baby girl? Would you like a ride to our neighbors' place?"

Marisa smiled and waved her arms.

"I thought you'd like that." Jane drove down the highway and turned west on the next county road.

Penny Long seemed happy to see them and invited them inside. She offered Jane iced tea.

"May I hold the baby?" Penny asked, stretching out her arms.

"Sure." Jane smiled at Marisa, who looked momentarily alarmed when Penny took her. "It's all right, baby girl," Jane crooned. Marisa appeared reassured and promptly became fascinated with Penny's dangling earrings.

Jane looked around. The kitchen seemed different. It took a moment before Jane identified the change. The Longs had replaced their avocado refrigerator and range with new white models. Jane, whose harvest gold–colored appliances dated from the same decade as Penny's, wished she could replace hers.

"I like your new appliances," Jane said.

"Aren't they great? I just love them. They use only a fraction of the electricity the old ones did. You should replace yours, too, to save energy."

"I wish I could afford to replace them."

"Shoot, with the extra money you get from your campers, you could. Tom got a real good deal on these in Marfa."

"Maybe after I pay off my bank loan."

"Yeah, those bank loans are awful. Nearly killed my dad before he got free and clear. Worked two jobs for years." Worriedly, she added, "Tom's working in town part-time."

"I didn't know that," Jane said.

"Yeah. A couple of nights a week. He promised he'd do it only until we pay off some of the things we bought."

Working part-time, it would take a long while to pay off a truck and new appliances, Jane thought, but she said nothing.

"Say, Jane, would you like the girls' baby clothes for Marisa?"

"If you're sure you won't need them again."

Penny laughed. "I'm sure. Tom says three girls is more than enough. I was going to call you and ask, and then send the box with Christie next time she babysat for you."

"That's why I stopped by. I'm wondering if Christie could babysit this weekend. We have another camping party."

"I'm sure she can. She's saving money to pay for cosmetology school. And let me tell you, that girl can save with a capital *S*. Me, I couldn't hold on to a dollar bill if my life depended on it."

As Jane left the Long ranch, she wondered where it was that Tom did his moonlighting to pay for all the improvements she saw around the place.

"You are very quiet this evening," Santiago said.

Jane paused in the act of folding Marisa's diapers into precise thirds. "I thought you liked quiet women."

"I do, but you are very silent even for a quiet woman."

"I have much on my mind."

"The bank loan." He watched her nod. "Jane, even if this particular bank turns you down, there are others. It's not as if you had no collateral. You're building the ranch back up. You own land. Stock markets may crash, and paper profits may disappear, but the land remains. It is real. It endures."

Jane looked at Santiago with wonder in her eyes. She'd had no idea that he understood how she felt about the land. Not many people did. Her husband hadn't. She swallowed, trying to ease the tightness in her throat. If she wasn't careful, she might shed a few tears. She, who despised weeping women.

"Have you always lived here?" Santiago asked.

"Not always. My mother was born here, and when it was time for me to be born, she came back. And she returned when she got sick. She came back here to die."

"How old were you when your mother died?"

"Ten."

"I am sorry."

"Thank you," Jane whispered, touched by the compassion she saw in his tawny eyes.

"And you stayed?"

"With my grandfather. My dad came to visit between rodeo engagements and whatever else he was doing until he was killed, doing what he loved best. Just like Roy."

"Your husband also rodeoed?"

"Yes," she answered without elaborating. "Grandpa insisted I go to college, but when the other students went to Padre Island for spring break, I came here. I spent my summers at the ranch, helping out."

When Jane stopped speaking, he prompted, "When you got married?"

"We followed the rodeos, but I came back whenever I could. And when Roy was killed, I moved back."

"With your grandfather?"

"Yes."

"And you stayed even after he died and you were alone?" he asked, marveling at her strength, at the depth of her love for this land.

"Why not? I always felt at home here."

"You are lucky to have such deep roots to anchor you."

He had lost his home, his country, his roots. "I'm so sorry," she murmured. "You've lost everything."

"Not everything," he said softly. "I have my life, and I have Marisa." Then he shook his head. "I didn't mean to make you sad." Casting around for a way to cheer her up, he remembered something. "I saw some boxes in the pantry next to the typewriter. Are they board games?"

"They are."

Santiago went into the pantry. When he returned a minute later, he held up a box with a smile.

"Scrabble? I haven't played that since Grandpa died five years ago."

"Time to play again." Santiago set up the game. "You go first." He placed the dictionary between them and smiled at her.

Chapter Six

The weekend passed uneventfully except for one small incident. After the guests had left on Sunday afternoon, Jane turned to Santiago, her forehead wrinkled in a frown.

"There was one more person with the campers this afternoon than there was on Friday. I counted twice, so I'm pretty sure I didn't make a mistake."

"You didn't," Santiago said.

"You counted them too?"

"I noticed the extra man."

"Where did he come from?"

"The other side of the river. That's my guess," Santiago said.

"An illegal? He crossed some really rough terrain to get to the mesa."

"It can be done. The harder part is after the illegals cross the border. They have to evade the border patrols and not get lost before they find water and food. Of course, it's easier if they get flown to the mesa and then join a camping party."

Jane shook her head with obvious disgust. "Is everybody but us involved in smuggling? This was a completely different set of campers from Susan Baldwin's guests."

Quietly Santiago said, "The people taking care of the campers were the same."

"You mean Leanne? I can't believe she'd be part of anything illegal," Jane said, her voice firm.

Though he admired Jane's loyalty to her friend, he had to make her aware of all the possibilities. "Leanne is only one person. She has several men helping her."

"The wranglers and Byron?" Jane considered his words for a moment. "The wranglers, maybe. But Byron? He strikes me as too lazy and too weak to get involved in something like that. It's too much like work."

"But the money is good. That might tempt even a lazy man."

"You have a point," she conceded. "Darn. I hate to think that they're using Leanne. Especially that Byron is using her. She's a good, decent, hardworking woman. She doesn't deserve being deceived and used."

"But isn't the alternative worse?"

"That she is a willing accomplice? Yes, it is," Jane agreed, her expression unhappy. Looking toward the house, she said, "I'd better go in so the babysitter can go home. Christie's working part-time at the Beauty Shoppe tomorrow after school."

"Wait," Santiago said. He had to make a phone call from town. He didn't want to use Jane's phone for fear that the wrong people would trace it back to the ranch. He couldn't, wouldn't, involve her any deeper than he absolutely had to. Every time he thought of his ex-compadre getting his hands on Jane, sweat beaded on his forehead. Santiago fisted his hands until his knuckles turned white. Forcing himself to be calm, he said, "The Fourth of July is coming up soon. Does the town celebrate the holiday?"

"Oh, yes. There's usually a parade, booths with food, music, and fireworks. Would you like to go? Heaven knows I owe you time off," Jane said, looking guilty. "I should have insisted on your taking a day off each week."

"I'd like to go, but not by myself. I wouldn't know what to do. I've never been to an Independence Day celebration." He paused, hoping she'd offer to go with him. When she didn't, he added, his tone low-key, "Why don't you come with me? It'll take our minds off banks and Immigration and smugglers. We could leave after we feed the animals. Wouldn't that get us to town in time for the fireworks and some food?"

"It would," she agreed cautiously.

Sensing that he had her half convinced, Santiago added,

"This might be my only chance to take part in a Fourth of July ceremony. And you haven't had a day off since I've been at the ranch."

"I guess if we go after the evening chores are done—"

"Then it's settled." He could make his phone call and spend leisure time with Jane. It occurred to him that this was sort of a date. He smiled. When he became aware of his reaction, he mentally shook his head. Surely he was old enough that a date with a woman should not fill him with such joyful anticipation—and yet it did.

Jane regarded her mirror image critically. Did the hem hang evenly? She had let it out because the skirt had seemed frivolously short to her. She turned, watching the green and blue flower-sprigged fabric swirl around her legs. Perfect for dancing. With a little catch in her breathing, she imagined Santiago twirling her, then drawing her back into his arms. Quickly she dismissed the appealing picture from her mind.

She didn't even know if Santiago knew how to dance. A lot of men didn't. And even if he did, he might not ask her. Or it wouldn't mean anything. Did she want the dance to have a special meaning? Of course not. She was just going with Santiago because he had never been to an Independence Day celebration. And, as he'd pointed out, this might be his only chance. As always, when she thought of his leaving, she felt dread settle heavily on her chest.

Don't invite trouble before it strikes. With a wry smile she recalled the countless times her grandfather had said those words to her. *Lighten up.* This was a festive occasion. How long had it been since she'd been out with a man?

This was not a date, she reminded herself. A good thing, too, since she didn't know how a thirty-year-old woman was supposed to behave on a date. Casting one last glance at her image, Jane decided that she looked tidy and respectable—and that, after all, was what she'd aimed for. Glamorous or sexy or beautiful was definitely beyond her means.

Picking up Marisa's diaper bag, Jane joined Santiago, who

was waiting for her by the truck. He paused in the act of folding the stroller to look at her. She thought his eyes held an
approving gleam, but, reminding herself that she was prone to
jumping to conclusions, Jane suppressed the flicker of excitement that warmed her.

"Did you fasten the straps on Marisa's car seat?" she asked
unnecessarily, because she couldn't think of anything else to
say.

Santiago nodded. "She cannot tell me in words, but I think
she's excited about going to her first Fourth of July festivities,"
he said with a smile.

"She's excited anytime we go anywhere in the truck."

"That doesn't bode well for the future," Santiago said with
mock concern. "I can see her at fifteen, demanding the keys to
the car."

"Sixteen. At fifteen she'll be agitating for her learner's permit."

Santiago groaned. "By the time she's seventeen, my hair will
be white from worrying."

"I think you'll do just fine," Jane said. Though she didn't
have much to go on, she knew in her heart that he would be a
good father. Was that part of what made him so attractive to
her? Probably. That and the fact that he exuded a sexy male
aura that called to her powerfully on a very basic female level.
What a lethal combination. No wonder it took all her willpower to remain immune to it. Not immune—not when she
was so aware of him every minute of every day—but at least
resistant to it.

By the time they reached town and found a parking place, they
had missed the speeches. Jane didn't think that was a great
loss. They watched the parade.

"I think Marisa likes the bands," Santiago said, holding the
baby up so she could see. "I shouldn't be surprised. Both her
parents loved music. My sister had a fine soprano voice."

"Did you hear that, baby girl? You'll probably sing in the
choir and play an instrument in the marching band," Jane said
to the baby. "Look, there's your babysitter."

"Christie?" Santiago looked at the members of the high school band passing before them. "The third trombone player in the second row?" he asked, somewhat hesitatingly. When Jane nodded, he added, "I wouldn't have recognized her in the uniform."

Jane chuckled. "Aren't those uniforms ugly? We wore the same ones when I marched in the band."

"Oh? What instrument did you play?"

"The trumpet. And before you ask, I wasn't very good at it. Actually, the only reason I was in the band was that the band director needed every student who could hold an instrument. My school wasn't very large." Jane glanced at her watch. "Why don't we follow the parade to the town square and get something to eat?"

Thirty minutes later Jane wiped her hands on a paper napkin. "I can't eat another thing except maybe a small part of an elephant ear. Will you share one with me?"

"Of course," Santiago said with a smile. Assuming a mock serious expression, he added, "I hope you noticed how much I trust you."

Puzzled, Jane asked, "Trust me? I don't understand."

"Without blinking an eye I agreed to eat something that I don't have a clue about. Moreover, it sounds sort of . . . What is the word Christie always uses? Gross?"

Jane laughed. "Taken literally, eating an elephant ear is sort of gross. Don't worry, though. The kind I have in mind is a large, thin pastry covered with sugar and cinnamon. It's really good. I promise."

Looking into her eyes, Santiago said, "I believe you. I trust you. I am sure you won't lead me into a gastronomic disaster."

"'Gastronomic disaster'?" Jane chuckled and shook her head. "You sure have a way with words. And English isn't even your native language. I still think you should try your hand at writing."

"I've been thinking about that."

Jane stopped in the middle of the street. "And?"

"I think you are right. I have been toying with several plots in my mind."

Jane felt joy flood through her. Why Santiago's words should please her so, she didn't know. "How exciting. Any evening you want to put those plots onto paper, you know where the typewriter is."

"Thanks. I have been meaning to ask you if I could use it."

"Feel free." Would he let her read his story? She assumed that writing had to be very personal, had to reveal a good deal about the writer, even if only obliquely. Yet from all she'd read, writers were eager to have their stories published and read, risking rejection and criticism. Jane didn't understand that, but then, she was a rancher, not a writer.

After a woman bumped into her, Jane resumed crossing the street. She purchased an elephant ear, broke off a piece, and handed the rest to Santiago. She watched him closely as he tasted it. He took a second bite, a third, and still he didn't say anything.

"Well?" she demanded, a little worried.

"Um," he murmured, chewing with a thoughtful expression.

Quickly Jane took a bite from her pastry, wondering if the vendor had produced an elephant ear of inferior quality. It tasted fine to her. Confused, she looked at Santiago. The roguish grin he lavished on her made her breath catch.

"Delicious," he murmured.

Playfully, she tapped him on the arm. "Keeping me wondering wasn't very nice," she scolded, trying not to smile.

"But fun. You could stand a little fun in your life."

"And you couldn't?"

"True. It's been a long time since I have balanced my life between work and enjoyment," he admitted.

"On the ranch there isn't much to do in the way of fun." She shrugged apologetically.

"We seem to be holding up traffic," he said, looking at the crowd trying to buy elephant ears. Pulling Jane by the hand, he pushed the stroller behind the nearest vendor's booth. Satisfied that they were hidden from view, Santiago laid his hands on Jane's shoulders. "You are wrong about there not being anything to do in the way of enjoyment at the ranch."

She made the mistake of looking into his tawny eyes. A mixture of alarm and excitement coursed through her. "Scrabble?" she asked. Her voice sounded faint and breathless, as if she'd run a mile.

"Playing with words is enjoyable but ultimately somewhat unsatisfactory."

Before Jane could say anything, he framed her face with his hands.

"Hold still. There's a bit of sugar caught in the corner of your mouth."

Jane's immediate impulse was to raise her hands to her mouth, but Santiago prevented her.

"Let me," he murmured.

His voice flowed over her like a caressing growl, and the gleam in his eyes caused a small tremor to skitter down her spine. She ought to say something, ought to stop him from doing any of the dark, dangerous, delicious things that hot gleam promised, yet she remained not only mute but lifted her face for his kiss in breathless expectation.

Long, hot minutes later, Marisa's gurgling voice broke them apart.

"The little one doesn't like to be ignored," Santiago murmured.

"No, she doesn't," Jane agreed. Thank heaven Marisa had demanded attention. Without the baby's interruption, Jane didn't know how long they would have kissed. She pushed the stroller back to the sidewalk.

Even though she was basically glad their kissing session had been interrupted, she felt just the tiniest twinge of disappointment. Talk about being ambivalent and conflicted.

They walked side by side. What was Santiago thinking? She glanced at him quickly, briefly. His face had assumed its habitual lack of expression.

"Over here!" someone called out.

Jane recognized Father Anselmo's voice hailing them. She

located him sitting at a picnic table. He waved for them to join him.

While Jane was busy lifting the baby from the stroller, Santiago and the padre exchanged a few words, too low for her to hear them.

"Excuse me for a few minutes," Santiago said, and he disappeared into the crowd.

"I don't suppose you want to tell me what that was about?" Jane asked.

"He's just getting us something to drink. He'll be back shortly," Father Anselmo said. "Let me hold the baby."

Jane suspected that the good father wasn't telling her the whole truth. But Santiago did return in a few minutes, carrying paper cups.

After they'd consumed their drinks, Santiago said, "Why don't we look at the booths? Want to join us, Father?"

"No, thanks. I've seen them already." They said their good-byes.

They admired the many wares displayed, but Jane didn't show a real interest in anything until they reached the booth displaying strings of beads, bracelets, and earrings. Most were colorful and inexpensive. Nestled amid the bright beads was a locket that made Jane catch her breath. Its design was simple. The golden oval was etched with a flower garland around its edge. Jane asked the vendor if she could take a closer look at it.

"How much?" she asked. When the man mentioned a price, Jane haggled, as he clearly expected her to do. Amiably they settled on a price.

"Isn't it lovely?" Jane held up the locket for Santiago to see. He sucked in his breath as if he'd received a blow to the stomach.

"May I?" he asked, his voice strained.

Jane handed him the pendant. He turned it over to look at the back. Wordlessly he returned it to her. "What?" she asked, alarmed by his expression.

Santiago addressed the vendor. Although Jane understood

some Spanish, she could not follow the rapid stream of words and questions Santiago flung at the man. Apparently not satisfied with the man's short, truculent answers, Santiago strong-armed him and quick-stepped him behind the canvas that formed the back wall of the booth.

Jane was so unprepared for this violent side to Santiago that she froze. As if through a dense, icy mist, she heard grunts, groans, and muttered curses. A minute or so later Santiago reappeared.

"Let's go home," he said, his voice curt.

"Is that man okay?" she asked, slanting a worried look back at the booth.

"He's better than he deserves to be."

"What does that mean?"

"It's a long story," Santiago said, his tone signaling his unwillingness to continue the discussion.

She wouldn't press him to relate a long story on the sidewalk, amid a crowd, but neither was she willing to let him totally off the hook.

"What if he calls the cops and presses charges? That won't go over well with the Immigration people."

"He won't say a word to the police or Immigration. Trust me on that. Let's get out of here."

Santiago was obviously in a hurry. Was he fearful that the vendor's friends would appear? Or the cops? Jane was still too appalled by the violent incident to say anything. Besides, Santiago looked utterly unapproachable.

They were silent all the way to the ranch. In her mind Jane kept replaying the scene at the vendor's booth. The words *el lobo* had been mentioned several times. *The wolf.* What did that mean?

After the baby had been put down for the night, she said, "Come to the kitchen. We have to talk."

Jane sat at the kitchen table, placed the pendant before her, folded her hands, and looked at Santiago expectantly.

"Why must we talk?" he asked, his tone weary.

Jane looked at him for a long moment. "You are too intelligent a man not to know why. You beat up that man. I need to know why."

"First of all, I didn't beat him up. All I did was a little arm-twisting."

"The difference between arm-twisting and beating up, if it exists, must be a male distinction. But we can skip that for now. Why did you have to twist his arm?"

"Because he wouldn't tell me the truth."

"About what?"

"You're not letting this go, are you?" Santiago asked, looking tired.

"Not until you give me some truthful answers. You're not the only one who wants the truth."

Santiago studied her, his dark eyes unreadable. Finally he nodded. "The locket you bought. It belonged to my sister. Corazon wore it when she was killed in an ambush."

Jane's right hand flew to her throat. "How awful," she whispered. "No wonder you were so distraught. You were there too." She paused, trying to take that in.

Jane would have questions, and Santiago had to decide how much he should tell her. If he told her too little, she wouldn't be satisfied, wouldn't trust him. If he told her too much, she might be in danger from his former comrades-in-arms who had turned to drug smuggling.

"How did the locket end up here?" she asked.

"The men who ambushed us are smugglers. They do business on both sides of the border."

"Is this the same ambush in which Paco lost his wing?"

"Yes." He looked at her, surprised. "I forgot that I told you that."

"Was the vendor one of the men who ambushed you?"

"It all happened so fast," he said, remembering, and while remembering, he relived the pain and the terror. He gripped the edge of his chair. "If he wasn't a member of that group, he certainly knew them. He admitted as much."

"Can you tell me about the ambush? Where and when did it

happen?" She watched him as he debated what he should tell her.

He sat down, and in a completely unemotional voice he told her how bandits had ambushed them, how he had been wounded, how everyone except the baby and him had been killed.

Jane was shocked into silence. She couldn't think of a single appropriate thing to say. The way he had told her, in that matter-of-fact manner, showed her more clearly than words ever could how deep his pain was, how far from coming to terms he was with what had happened.

Finally she laid a hand on his in a comforting gesture, but Santiago didn't seem to notice. It was not until she pressed his hand that he became aware of his surroundings.

He rose and walked to the window. Staring out into the darkness, he seemed heartbreakingly alone. Jane followed him.

"How did you survive? How did you find the willpower to go on?" she asked softly.

"The baby. If it hadn't been for Marisa, I'm not sure I would have bothered dragging myself out of that jungle."

"I know what you mean. If my grandfather hadn't needed me, I don't know how I would have gone on after my husband was killed." Roy hadn't been a model husband, but she had loved him. At least in the beginning. Though theirs hadn't been the happiest of marriages, his death had hit her hard.

Santiago looked at her and nodded. "We're both survivors," he said, and he turned again toward the darkness outside. "There is something you need to know. I *will* avenge Corazon. Nothing will stop me."

Jane nodded. That was something a man like him would do. She didn't really understand revenge or retribution, but even if he hadn't said so, she would instinctively know that a man like Santiago would be compelled to avenge his sister.

"What is it you see out there?" she asked.

"Ghosts. Memories. Hopes. Regrets. Broken dreams."

Jane knew all about those.

Turning to her, he attempted a smile. "Aren't you sorry you asked?"

"No. What you've told me explains some things about you."

"Such as?"

"The dark, violent side of you I saw tonight."

Santiago wrapped his arms around her. Laying his cheek against her hair, he murmured, "Ah, *querida*, you have no idea about the violence in my life. Or the darkness in my soul."

Jane knew pain and loss and loneliness. She knew the dangers of rodeo life. She knew death. But violence?

"No, I don't understand violence. I doubt that I ever will." Jane touched the scar that ran from high on his forehead into his thick black hair. "Did you get this in the ambush?"

"Yes. I've been told that a plastic surgeon might be able to lessen its repulsiveness."

"I don't find it repulsive." Jane rose on tiptoe to place a kiss on the scar.

Santiago swayed. No woman's kiss, not even the most passionate, had ever affected him so deeply. He felt a searing ache in his throat. Repressed tears? He hadn't felt those since he'd used his bare hands to dig a shallow grave for his sister. He pulled Jane closer and laid his forehead against hers.

"You must have been in so much pain. No doctor, no medication. And the devastating loss of your sister and your companions," she said, her voice low, empathetic.

Santiago's throat hurt so much, he couldn't speak. It took several seconds before he could pull himself together. Finally he managed to say, "I had my hands full, caring for Marisa, foraging for food, and finding our way to a safe village. I didn't have time to notice the pain of my wounds."

"There were more than one?"

He shrugged. "A bullet grazed my side and injured a couple of ribs."

Jane squeezed her eyes shut, trying to stop the tears but failing. She kissed him softly on the mouth.

Santiago's hands latched on to the windowsill behind him. Better to grab the wood than Jane. If he touched her, all would be lost. He'd be tempted to forget the oath he'd sworn at Corazon's grave, tempted to let a great wrong go unpunished, tempted to bury his need for revenge and retribution. A woman's tears, a woman's soft touch, a woman's caring, sympathetic, and understanding heart were more dangerous than a dozen enemies with semiautomatic weapons.

Besides, he had nothing to offer Jane. He was homeless, his face and body were scarred, and he was consumed with the need for meting out justice. Jane deserved so much more than that.

Gently, he brushed the tears from her face. "Thank you for your tears. It's been a long time since a woman cried over me. Good night, Jane."

Quickly, before he could change his mind, he went to his room and closed the door.

Chapter Seven

Jane woke early, her heart hammering with anxiety. Her dreams had been filled with images of Santiago in danger. Unwilling to risk a continuation of the dreams should she fall asleep again, Jane rose, dressed, and started her morning chores in the barn. Only minutes later, Santiago joined her.

"I'm sorry if I woke you. I tried to be quiet."

"You were. I'm a light sleeper. And I didn't sleep well either."

They exchanged a look of understanding. No words were necessary.

They fed and groomed the horses. While Santiago finished cleaning the stalls, Jane fed the chickens and collected the eggs. She took a quick shower. By the time Santiago had shaved and showered, she had breakfast ready.

"Are you upset with me?" he asked after finishing his pancakes.

"No. Why would you think that?"

"You've hardly said ten words this morning."

"Do I usually chatter?"

Santiago laid a hand on her arm as she refilled his coffee cup. "No, you don't." He studied her face.

"Do you find my silence disapproving?" she asked.

"No," he conceded.

"But?" she prompted.

"But the way you referred to my violent side last night felt . . . disapproving."

Jane nodded. "I don't approve of violence. It doesn't solve problems."

"I agree. But sometimes violence is not avoidable. Jane, I don't go out looking for fights."

"But you don't run from them either."

"Running from them doesn't necessarily solve problems either."

Jane set the coffeepot on the counter. She turned and looked at him, giving him all of her attention.

"My life during the past five years or so has been filled with violence. I don't deny that. I didn't go looking for violence. But I was faced with the choice of fighting to stay alive or not fighting and dying. I chose to stay alive."

"As you should have. Life is definitely preferable. I'm glad you fought to stay alive," she added softly.

"Me too."

Just then they heard Marisa's first demanding cries.

"Sounds like someone is ready for breakfast," Jane said with a smile.

"I'll get her."

Jane removed the muslin cover from the birdcage and listened to Paco's raucous morning chatter. "Do you stay awake at night thinking of all those words?" she asked.

"Baby, baby. Paco. Paco."

"Paco, *silencio,*" Santiago admonished.

The bird decided to groom himself.

"Have you noticed that Paco usually talks when we eat?" Jane asked.

"Yes. He hopes he'll get a treat."

"He usually does. Smart bird."

While Santiago fed the baby, Jane looked at the newspaper she had picked up in town.

"This is interesting," she said. "A long article about the INS cracking down on fake marriages. Remember Deputy Wilson talking about that?"

Santiago nodded. "I believe his exact words were that if an alien could 'persuade some gullible U.S. female citizen to marry him,' he could remain in this country."

"Apparently that's been happening quite often."

"Under certain circumstances that might be a workable solution," Santiago said nonchalantly. He didn't look at Jane but focused his attention on feeding Marisa.

Jane regarded him thoughtfully. "Maybe, but according to this article, Mrs. Winter, the INS official in charge of this part of Texas, will make these marriages of convenience very difficult, if not impossible. She sounds tough and positively *wintry*."

Santiago chuckled at Jane's play on words.

Jane turned back to the front page and frowned. "Maybe we should turn on the television once in a while to watch the news."

"Why? What happened?"

"Someone tried to shoot the governor. Apparently he's been receiving threats from some fringe group. They suspect that the would-be assassin was a foreigner who apparently entered the States illegally. Probably by way of Mexico."

"Did they catch him?"

"They shot him. Here's a photo of him."

Santiago studied the photo intently.

"Does he look familiar to you?" Jane asked.

"Yes."

"To me too, but I have no earthly idea where I could have seen him." Jane stared at the photo a moment longer before she folded the newspaper. "Time to exercise the horses. We have a weekend party to get ready for."

"I'll change Marisa, and then I'll join you," Santiago said.

As soon as Jane was out the door, he reached for the phone. Santiago hated to call from the ranch, but he had no choice. This was important, for he knew exactly where he'd seen the assassin. He was the extra man in the camping party.

When Santiago brought in the mail at noon, he saw the letter from the bank. He didn't say anything as he placed the stack of mail on the counter. If the news was bad, Jane might be too upset to eat. They had worked hard repairing a section of the east fence, and Jane needed food to replenish her strength.

"How about some music?" Santiago asked. "The announcer promised a selection of Bach for the noon concert."

"Sure," Jane said. "I've lived here most of my life, and until you came, I never knew we had a classical station in the area." Jane plated the short ribs, carrots, and potatoes she had cooked in the Crock-Pot.

Santiago waited until they'd sated their hunger before he spoke. "I need to go to the mesa with the camping party this weekend. Can you think of a way I could do that without arousing suspicion?"

Surprised, Jane put her fork down. "Several times in the past, when Leanne was shorthanded, one of my hands would go along to help. He'd give up his day off, and she would pay him. The hands liked getting the extra income." Jane stopped, obviously hesitant to go on. "I could call Leanne and tell her that you'd be willing to do that."

Santiago noticed her lack of enthusiasm. "But you don't like the idea. Why?"

"It could be dangerous. What if they catch you snooping?"

"I wouldn't 'snoop.' Just keep my eyes and ears open." He could tell she still didn't like the idea, but she nodded.

"I'll call Leanne right now."

While Jane made the call, Santiago finished feeding Marisa. When he came back from putting her down for a nap, Jane stood looking out the kitchen window, the letter from the bank in her hand. From her posture, he could tell that the news was not good.

"What did the banker say?" he asked.

"That he regrets not being able to renew my loan."

"I'm so sorry, Jane."

"What am I going to do?" she whispered.

Sensing that she was close to tears, Santiago put his arms around her and held her.

"I could lose my home."

"No, you won't. There are lots of banks out there. We'll start with Odessa, Midland, and El Paso. If that doesn't work, we'll go farther east. We'll start making lists tonight and phone calls tomorrow."

"I hate to beg."

"You won't be begging. If banks didn't make loans, they'd go out of business. They make a good profit from each loan. They need you as much as you need them. Believe me." Santiago kissed her hair. He loved the way it smelled of sunshine.

Responding to the caress, Jane threw caution to the wind. She was so tired of being cautious, levelheaded, and reticent. She wound her arms around his neck and kissed him. Startled, Santiago hesitated only for a moment before he responded to the sweet touch of her lips. He had been wanting to kiss Jane again ever since they'd kissed on Independence Day. Though he had long dreamed of tasting her lips, he had not suspected there would be such magic, such urgency, such heat, in her kiss. Passion built quickly, hotly. Before it could spiral out of control, Santiago pulled back.

"Jane," he murmured, "this is not a good idea." Seeing the stricken look on her face, he quickly added, "Don't misunderstand. There's nothing I'd like more. But you're vulnerable right now. You've suffered a major disappointment. I won't take advantage of your vulnerability, because later you might regret it. I'd hate that. Come to me anytime you're not so down, *querida*."

He stroked her hair. "Now I have to go before I change my mind. Part of me is going to regret walking away from you. I'm sure I'll end up calling myself a fool in at least three languages."

Santiago left with the camping party on Friday. Twenty-four hours later, the silence closed in on Jane. Even Paco was quiet in his cage. That silence suddenly felt uncomfortable surprised her. For years she had lived contentedly with silence. Now she found it unnerving. With Marisa on her lap, she phoned Father Anselmo.

After exchanging a bit of small talk, Jane said, "Santiago went up to the mesa with the campers."

After a moment's silence, Father Anselmo said, "And this worries you."

"Yes. It could be dangerous. Doesn't it worry you?"

"I have faith that Santiago knows what he's doing."

"Getting back to the question of danger. There's one thing I've been worrying about."

"Just one thing, Jane? I'm surprised."

Jane could picture his smile. She rolled her eyes. "I'm serious, Father. If something were to happen to Santiago, God forbid, what would happen to Marisa? She wouldn't have to be put into the foster care system, would she?"

"I can hear the fear in your voice, but don't worry. Marisa would not go into foster care. Santiago signed a document, giving me custody."

"That's good, and I know you're fond of her, but how could you take care of a baby?" Jane asked.

"I'd have to find a good woman to do that."

Jane swallowed hard. "A 'good woman'? I don't know if I qualify, but—"

"You qualify. We were both thinking of you when Santiago signed the document."

Jane felt a load of rocks roll off her heart. "Thank you. You don't know how much I appreciate knowing I could keep her safe and sound."

"About the danger, have a little confidence and trust in the man. I know that's not easy for you, but try," he said.

"Father, are you implying I have trust issues?"

"It would be surprising if you didn't, what with your father as well as your late husband hardly qualifying as models of responsibility and reliability. They were men who always put themselves and their pleasures first."

"And Santiago isn't like that?"

"What do you think?"

"I know he puts Marisa first," Jane said.

"But?"

"But there's a darkness in him I don't understand. Something from his past."

"I know. We can only pray and hope that time will banish the darkness from his soul." Father Anselmo paused. Very gently he added, "Give him time. He's much better than he was when he first came to me." He paused again. "Jane, your feelings for Santiago. How deep are they?"

She thought for a moment. Softly she said, "I'm not sure, but deeper than they ought to be."

"I think you're sure, Jane."

Hearing the mild rebuke in his voice, Jane felt a swift stab of guilt. She hadn't lied to the padre. She just wasn't ready to examine her heart and face her feelings. "Are you warning me not to . . . have feelings for Santiago?"

"Would it do any good?" he asked.

Jane didn't answer.

"Your silence tells me that it wouldn't. In truth, I'm not sure whether I should warn you or not."

"You like him, don't you, Father?"

"Yes. But he comes with lots of emotional baggage from his past."

"So do I," Jane pointed out.

"True. No one can escape the burdens of the past. Part of life." Then he chuckled.

"What's so amusing?" Jane asked. "I could use a laugh."

"Remember what I warned you about a couple of months ago?"

"Ha! Which warning are you talking about?"

"The one where I told you that if you didn't let people back into your life, you'd dry up and blow away like a tumbleweed."

"Yes, I recall that particular conversation."

"Well, now at least I won't have to worry about that anymore. Peace, Jane."

Thoughtfully Jane hung up the phone. The good padre was right. Shocked, she realized how much she had come to love Marisa. She kissed the baby's soft black hair. And Santiago? She couldn't imagine living without him.

This was not good. What had happened to the self-sufficiency, the independence, she'd prided herself on? Gone. It was all gone. Father Anselmo would probably tell her it was a good thing she was no longer such a loner who needed no one. Or thought she didn't.

Then she came back to the question that was haunting her dreams as well as her waking moments: what if Santiago couldn't stay in this country? Jane's arms tightened around the baby. She couldn't lose them. She had only just found them. There had to be a way to keep them. There just had to.

To distract her from her worrisome thoughts, Jane painted the floor of the front porch. While she stood behind the screen door admiring the shiny slate-gray surface, a patrol car drove up. At first she thought it might be Bud Wilson again, coming to check up on Santiago, but it wasn't.

Physically, Sheriff Ryback was the opposite of his deputy. Taciturn, reserved, and tall and thin to the point of gauntness, he had always intimidated her a little. Maybe it was his eyes— small, ferrety, almost colorless. Or the fact that he never smiled.

Jane opened the screen door. "I'm sorry, Sheriff, but I can't ask you in. I just painted the porch, and it isn't dry yet."

"Looks good," he said. He turned slowly and looked at the corral and the barn.

"As busy as you are, I know this isn't a social visit," she said. "What can I do for you?"

"I just stopped by to see if everything's okay."

He had never done that before. He hadn't even come when she'd asked him but had sent his deputy instead. "Everything's fine, though we could use some rain."

He glanced at the sky. "Yeah. Sure could. Your new hand. He's out working the range?"

"Yes."

He nodded. "Well, I'd better be off, Mrs. Peterson." He raised a hand to his hat, got back into the car, and drove off.

Jane watched until the patrol car was out of sight. With a frown, she wondered why she hadn't told him that Santiago was up on the mesa. Maybe because the sheriff made her uneasy? She shrugged. He kept being elected, so he had to do his job reasonably well, and being friendly and personable surely wasn't in his job description.

* * *

The letter from the Immigration office came in Saturday's mail. Jane examined the envelope, wishing she were psychic so she could divine its contents. With a sigh, she placed it on top of the radio. She would have to wait until Santiago came home.

The camping party returned to the ranch on Sunday afternoon. Jane exchanged a few words with Leanne, who looked exhausted, the dark rings under her eyes hinting at sleeplessness. Byron, sitting on the hood of one of the trucks and looking bored, smoked a cigarette. Jane clamped her teeth together to keep from telling him to get off his sorry rump and help. Why did Leanne put up with him? Was she that smitten with him? True, he had a sort of sulky, sneering handsomeness, but that didn't compensate for his basic laziness. At least in Jane's opinion, it didn't.

As soon as the last truck pulled out, Santiago picked up Marisa, who had been watching from the safety of her playpen on the porch. The baby squealed with delight when her uncle lifted her into the air.

"She missed you," Jane said.

"Did you miss me too?"

Did she ever! Jane nodded. Aloud she said, "It was so quiet around here, I had to call Father Anselmo just to hear an adult voice."

"How's the good father?"

"Full of advice as always."

Santiago laughed.

His teeth flashed white against his sun-bronzed skin. He looked good despite the fact that he hadn't shaved in a couple of days. Or maybe because of it? The unshaven look lent him a dangerous, rakish air that made Jane's toes curl.

"What did you find out on the mesa?" she asked.

"All the trucks have false bottoms. Deep enough to hide contraband but not deep enough to be obvious."

"False bottoms?" Jane collapsed onto the porch swing. "Thank heaven they're not Leanne's trucks. She rents them. Any idea what was under the false floors?"

"Semiautomatic weapons."

"Oh, no!" Jane whispered. "That's even worse than smuggling drugs." She paused. "I think." She paused again, trying to come to terms with the information. "Who'll get these weapons?"

"Could be any of a number of groups. Rebels, drug lords, insurgents, terrorists."

"This keeps getting worse and worse." Jane gripped the edge of the swing. "How did they get the weapons up the mesa? The last part of the trail is too steep for vehicles."

"Packhorses."

"What do you mean, packhorses? We don't have any pack animals."

"Someone else does. A man was waiting for the trucks with three packhorses," Santiago said.

"That's not possible. He would have had to go right past this house. I would have seen him."

"My guess is that he went across your neighbor's range and then crossed over to yours just below the mesa."

"Did you recognize him?" she asked.

"I've never seen him before."

"I'll ask Penny Long tomorrow if she saw anyone."

"Please don't."

"Why not?" Jane asked, puzzled. "Surely you want to catch . . ." She paused when the implication of his words hit her. "The Longs? No way. They can't be involved with smuggling."

"Why not? Couldn't they use the money?"

Jane opened her mouth to protest and then snapped it shut. She remembered all those new appliances and the new truck she had seen at the Long ranch. Penny had told her that Tom was working part-time in town, but it would take him years to pay for the things they'd acquired. "I can't believe Penny would condone arms smuggling."

"She may know nothing about it."

Jane looked mutely at Santiago. When she could, she said, "We have to stop the smuggling."

"I'm trying, *querida*. I couldn't stop this shipment from leaving, but now that I know how they do it, it'll be their last."

"And you will stop them? One man?"

"I'll certainly try."

"Why not go to the police?"

"The local sheriff and his deputy? They'd be no match for these men."

Santiago was probably right, but that did not lessen her fear for him.

Jane held out her arms for the baby. "The letter we've been waiting for came. It's on the radio."

Jane soothed the baby, who was ready for her nap, but Jane couldn't wait to find out what the letter said. She followed him into the kitchen. His expression, as stoic as she'd ever seen it, didn't tell her anything. Fearing the worst, she sat down.

Santiago looked at her. "They didn't extend my visa. Marisa and I have to leave the country in less than two weeks."

"No!" Her vehement cry alarmed the baby. Jane stroked Marisa's hair, murmuring soft words. "I'm going to put her down for her nap. Then we'll talk about this."

Santiago had expected Immigration to deny his petition. Filing for it had been a long shot. He knew some people with enough power to pull strings on his behalf, but that might expose him. He hadn't finished what he needed to do. He hadn't punished Corazon's murderers yet.

Time for Plan B—a plan he'd worked on unceasingly, thought about endlessly, and rehearsed repeatedly, but now that it was time to implement it, he was surprised to discover that his mouth was as dry and parched as the high mesa.

He'd faced numerous enemies without feeling trepidation, so why should one soft-spoken woman cause his hands to shake? Because he'd broken one cardinal rule: he'd let her get to him. *Damn.*

Jane came back in record time. She sat down, facing him. "This just isn't our week, is it? We both got turned down. What are we going to do?"

Here goes. "We can help each other. Solve each other's problem." Her cinnamon-colored eyes looked at him uncomprehendingly. Then they widened. She remembered.

"Deputy Wilson mentioned a way I could stay in this country even if Immigration denied my petition."

"Yes, but—"

"But how can I help you with the bank loan? I can pay it off."

"It's nice of you to offer, but I owe the bank lots of money." She handed him the letter from the bank and watched him read it. "You have that much money lying around?"

"Actually, I do. In a Swiss bank." Santiago watched the first hint of concern appear on her lovely face. Quickly he added, "I got the money legitimately. The nature of my work didn't allow me to get to a bank regularly, so I had my employer deposit my salary in a Swiss account."

Jane blinked.

He could tell she had trouble processing that.

"Who was your employer?" she asked.

"An agency of the U.S. government."

"Oh." She thought for a moment. "Then why can't this agency persuade Immigration to extend your visa? They're both agencies of the same government."

He hadn't anticipated that she'd think of that so readily. "That isn't how it works. My agency is secretive. They'll probably deny knowing me unless it's a matter of life and death."

"They're not very grateful, are they?"

Santiago chuckled. "Nobody ever accused them of being grateful. Jane, I do have the money. I can have it transferred to your bank in two or three days."

"You're really willing to lend me that amount?"

Santiago reached across the table and laid a hand on hers. "I'm willing to *give* that amount to my *wife*." He felt her hand jerk slightly.

" 'Wife'?"

She had said the word as if tasting it.

"If we get married, I can stay here. Marisa will have a chance to grow up in freedom and security. Was I wrong in assuming that you're fond of her?"

"I don't think I could bear to lose her," Jane said, her voice low. "It would break my heart."

"But you have reservations?"

"Don't you? We're talking marriage."

This was the difficult part. He had to persuade Jane without misleading her. He owed her that. He couldn't let her believe that he was offering undying, romantic love. First of all, he wasn't sure that there was such a thing as romantic love, and second, even if it existed, he wasn't sure he was capable of such feelings anymore. Somewhere in the jungles and the mountains he had lost the capacity for love. Everyone he had held dear and cared about had been killed. Death hadn't taken him. Only his ability to love.

He could offer loyalty, protection, and passion. Most women wouldn't think that was enough, but Jane might. Santiago inhaled deeply. He took both of her hands in his.

"We've both been married. We both married for romantic love. We both found out that that wasn't enough to make a marriage happy. Isn't that so?"

After a moment's hesitation, she nodded.

"You're thinking that maybe the second time around this might be different?"

She lowered her eyes briefly, telling him that she'd considered this.

"Jane, we've worked side by side and lived in the same house for weeks now. We get along. We like each other. Isn't that so?"

"Yes."

"We're also powerfully attracted to each other." He watched faint color seep into her cheeks. Intuitively he knew to back off a little from the topic of desire and passion. "We can make this marriage anything we want it to be. I suggest we start slowly. Continue as we are and see where that will lead us."

Santiago raised her hands and kissed each one. "Think about this. But remember that we don't have much time. We have to act fast." He rose. "I have to check on one of the horses. The palomino was favoring her left front leg."

At the door he stopped. "I don't mean to put pressure on you, but we have very little time left. Think fast, *querida.*"

Chapter Eight

Jane squirmed, pounded her pillow, and turned over count-less times, trying to fall asleep. Finally she resigned herself to spending the night staring at the ceiling. She replayed the scene with Santiago repeatedly. Everything he'd said made sense. Point by point.

Point one: she didn't have the money to pay off the bank loan. Cattle prices were way down, so even if she sold off her small herd, she would still come up short. Besides, she'd been working so hard to turn the place back into a cattle ranch that she just couldn't sell off her animals. She'd personally taken care of each one of them.

Point two: Immigration had refused to extend Santiago's visa. He'd have to leave in less than two weeks—with Marisa. Pain and anxiety knifed through Jane. She couldn't lose the baby. Or Santiago.

With a shudder, she recalled the barren years before the man and the baby had entered her life. She'd been able to en-dure the loneliness and the silence because she'd been numb inside. Maybe even dead. Rendered dead inside by her hus-band's violent death in the rodeo arena and by the loss of her grandfather to a heart attack only months later.

Jane couldn't go back to being dead inside. Not after allow-ing herself to feel again. Feel love for the baby, feel affection for Santiago, feel companionship and physical attraction. Strong physical attraction. Santiago made her feel like a woman again—a desirable woman.

Pressing the pillow over her face, Jane groaned. How could

93

she have allowed herself to feel so deeply so quickly? It was one thing to want to be part of the human community once more and quite another to become so deeply involved. So emotionally needy. So emotionally hungry.

She hadn't been careful. She had felt herself so far removed from ever feeling a woman's needs again for a family, a man, that she'd thought she would be forever immune. She had told herself for so long that she needed no one that she'd firmly convinced herself of that. Wrong. So very wrong.

Marriage would solve both their problems. Santiago's and hers. He would pay off her loan, and she would enable him to stay in this country indefinitely. A mutually beneficial bargain. Why was she even agonizing over the solution?

Don't, Jane. Just do it. Marry Santiago.

Jane swung her legs over the edge of the bed. A bed she might soon be sharing with Santiago? Her breath hitched. He'd proposed what amounted to a logical arrangement. A mutually beneficial arrangement. A contract. Even though they'd be married, everything would stay as it was. At least for a time.

She dressed quietly and went to the kitchen. As she started the coffee, Paco woke up in his cage.

"Baby, baby," he croaked.

"Paco, behave yourself," Santiago said, entering the kitchen. "Is he being a nuisance?"

"Not really." Jane watched Santiago fill two mugs with coffee. He handed her one. He leaned against the counter and sipped coffee.

"How did you sleep?" he asked.

"Fine," she said automatically. Then she shook her head. "I didn't sleep well. I had a lot to think about. A decision to make."

"Have you made a decision?" he asked, his voice quietly controlled.

"Yes."

Santiago waited, forcing himself to breathe. "What have you decided?"

"That you're right. Getting married will solve both of our problems. It's the logical thing to do."

Santiago's hand grasped the edge of the counter behind him to help him stay calm and controlled, when all he wanted was to shout a relieved and joyful *hallelujah*. Such a reaction would doubtlessly alarm Jane, who looked rather pale, her light brown eyes clouded with uncertainty and apprehension despite her outwardly calm demeanor. He guessed she had not made the decision to marry him easily or quickly.

His first impulse was to put his arms around Jane and hold her, but that gesture, meant to be physically reassuring, might make her even more uneasy. Instead he said, "Yes, it is the logical thing to do. It will be all right, Jane. You will see. Everything will work out just fine." She nodded.

"After we went to bed last night, it occurred to me that I forgot to mention one very important thing." He watched her hands tighten around the coffee mug.

"What?"

"A prenuptial agreement."

Jane stared at him silently. Finally she said, "I don't understand."

"You own this big ranch. You should protect it. I don't want you to lose a single acre of it, just in case you change your mind at some point in the future and want out of our marriage."

"Or you want out of it."

Santiago didn't think there was much chance of that happening, but he nodded. "I'll make some phone calls to find out what formalities are involved in getting married."

Jane nodded again.

"Any specific day you want to get married?"

"No. But I will have to make arrangements for a babysitter, so I'll need some advance notice."

"After morning chores are done, I'll make the calls." Santiago drained his mug. On the way to the door, he stopped. He couldn't just walk out so cold-bloodedly. Not after Jane had agreed to become his wife. He walked back to her. He cradled her face. He wanted to kiss her mouth, taste her, but hadn't he made the bold promise that they would take it slowly, keep the marriage one in name only? It occurred to him that he might have been excessively rash in making that promise.

He kissed her forehead and allowed himself to inhale the scent of her hair for a moment before he let her go.

After the chores and breakfast, Santiago phoned the ware-houselike compound in Maryland just outside the nation's capital. He didn't use the emergency number that would have connected him directly to the head of the Omega Group. That number was reserved for crises. Instead he spoke to the director's assistant—a woman who could have been the prototype heroine of the screwball comedy movies of the thirties.

Santiago suspected that Rosalee cultivated this image deliberately. Who would suspect that the seemingly featherbrained brunet behind the front desk of the run-down-looking company calling itself an import-export business was the right hand to the director of a powerful agency that often barely operated inside the law? An agency that tackled assignments no other official government office would touch?

"Rosalee, I need some information, and before you ask, it is not an emergency, but it is urgent." Santiago outlined what he had to know.

Fifteen minutes later he possessed everything he needed to draft a prenup agreement and knew what he had to do to get married in the State of Texas. He told Jane he would make all the arrangements. She didn't seem to mind. He thought she might even have been relieved.

When he told Jane two days later that they would get married within a week's time, he thought her lovely eyes widened just a bit, but otherwise she remained calm. Perhaps even a little stoic. He would have preferred a slightly more excited reaction, until he reminded himself that he was the one who had insisted on calling this marriage a business arrangement. What woman could get excited over that?

Chapter Nine

Santiago glanced at his silent bride. Jane had not uttered a word since she had said "I do." She seemed to concentrate on driving. Except there was little traffic, and such single-minded attention to the road was excessive.

He couldn't blame her for being silent. What was there to say? The ceremony had been brief and impersonal, the justice of the peace indifferent, the room bare and ugly. No music, no flowers, no friends. A strictly contractual procedure. The only personal touch had been the gold band he had asked Rosalee to mail by special overnight delivery.

Cursing silently, he berated himself for listening to Rosalee's instructions to keep the ceremony deliberately cold and impersonal. She had argued forcefully for keeping all sentiment out, as this would make it easier to annul the marriage later. Undoubtedly she was right. What Rosalee did not know was that Santiago was increasingly uncertain about returning to the Omega Group. Nor was he sure he would ever want his marriage to Jane annulled.

Maybe he should have consulted Father Anselmo. No. That would have been a huge mistake. It was going to be exceedingly difficult to explain the civil ceremony to the padre after the fact. Before the vows had been made, it would have been impossible. The man, after all, considered marriage sacred.

"We'd better stop and get supplies," Jane said. "It'll save us a trip back to town."

"Okay." Santiago eyed Jane warily. She sounded calm and normal. Maybe she had not been brooding over the marriage ceremony or her decision to marry him. He breathed easier.

"We're low on chicken feed," she said.

"We could use a couple of sacks of the special grain mixture Susan Baldwin wants for her horses."

Jane nodded. "And we're out of the pureed peaches Marisa likes so much."

"Maybe we'd better pick up a roll of barbed wire and posts for the south fence."

"That needs fixing again?" she asked with a frown.

"Yes. Some of the posts are rotted."

They stopped at the grocery store first. In the produce aisle, he felt Jane skid to a sudden stop.

"Oh, no," she whispered, laying a hand on Santiago's arm. "There's Father Anselmo. Helping blind Mrs. Cruz do her shopping."

"Just as well," Santiago said, patting her hand. "We had to tell him soon anyway."

Jane was so tense that when they greeted Father Anselmo, Santiago knew the padre had to notice.

"Are you two all right?" Father Anselmo asked.

Santiago smiled. "We are better than all right. Jane and I got married at the county seat this morning." He draped an arm over Jane's shoulders in a gesture that was protective and possessive. Maybe even a little defiant.

Father Anselmo was mute for several beats. Then, turning to Jane, he said, "Well, you warned me that one of these days you'd do something unexpected."

"Yes, I did," Jane admitted, her voice low.

"I thought you meant something relatively harmless, like changing your hair color," he added.

"You think marriage could be harmful?" Santiago asked.

"In some instances. When it's entered into lightly."

"Trust me, this marriage was anything but entered into lightly," Santiago said. He held the padre's gaze unwaveringly.

Father Anselmo sighed. Then he congratulated them and wished them well. With a smile but a serious voice he said to Jane, "You know I expect you to repeat your vows in church and before God one of these days. Just let me know when."

Watching the padre leave, Jane said, "He means that."

"I know he does. But we don't have to commit to a date right away."

Penny Long was sitting on the porch with Marisa on her lap when Jane stopped the truck in the Longs' yard.

"I'm going to tell her that we got married," Jane said to Santiago. "She's been a good neighbor for years. She'd be hurt if she heard it from someone else."

Santiago nodded. As they walked toward the porch, he took Jane's hand and squeezed it.

Judging by Penny's surprised expression, she had noticed the hand-holding. How could she have missed it? Santiago had not been furtive about it.

"Was Marisa a good little girl?" Jane asked, reaching for the baby.

"She was a very good girl. We had a great time. I'll watch her anytime you have an emergency," Penny said, her gaze flicking from Jane to Santiago. "What have you been up to?"

"Jane did me the honor of marrying me," Santiago said.

Penny's expression was one of classical, open-mouthed surprise. "Say that again?"

"We got married," Jane repeated.

"That's what I thought heard the first time," Penny said. "Well, I'll be."

Jane handed the baby to Santiago. "Why don't you put Marisa in her car seat while I get her things?" Jane asked, hoping Santiago would take the hint.

"All right." Santiago lifted Marisa high into the air. She cooed with pleasure.

"Her things are inside." Penny led the way into the kitchen. "Why didn't you tell me you were getting married? I'd have baked a cake."

"Thanks, but a cake isn't necessary. We wanted to keep this simple. Aren't you the one who urged me to get married again? Even marched a bunch of cowboys past me as possible husband material?"

Penny shrugged and grinned. "Yeah, I did. The ranch is too big for you to run by yourself. I didn't want you to get old and worn out before your time. Or kill yourself."

"It's amazing the difference one hardworking man makes," Jane admitted, her voice soft. "I baked lemon bars yesterday, something I hadn't had time to do since last winter."

"See? I told you that you needed a man in your life, and let's face it: Santiago is all man. He's got a sexy voice and accent. He's got lots of what my often-married Aunt Mamie called the old S.A. Sex appeal," Penny added. "Or in the lingo of my daughter and her friends, he's hot."

Jane nodded. To deny Santiago's sex appeal would be an out-and-out lie. But sex appeal was hardly a solid basis for a marriage. When she realized what she was worrying about, she stopped herself. Why was she agonizing about the solidity of this marriage? For all she knew, Santiago might want out of this union in three years' time when he became eligible for citizenship.

Three years might be all she'd have with him. Three years. A little over a thousand days. A thousand nights. Unbidden, the tale of Scheherazade and her one thousand and one nights popped into Jane's mind. Except Jane was no bewitching teller of tales who could enthrall her man.

"Is something wrong? You look so serious," Penny said.

Thank heaven Penny tore her out of those useless speculations. "I was just thinking of all we had to get done by Friday. We have another camping party coming through."

"No time for a honeymoon?"

Jane shook her head.

"Tom and I got married in June but had to wait until Christmas before we could get away from the ranch. You might want to consider the holidays too. Not a bad time to go to Padre Island or Cancun. I'll keep Marisa."

"That's sweet of you," Jane said, and she meant it. "We'll see." Jane picked up the diaper bag. "Where's Tom?"

"At his part-time job at the hardware store."

Penny walked out with Jane. They found Santiago and Marisa at the corral, looking at the horses.

"I don't remember seeing those three before," Jane said, nodding toward the horses.

"Tom bought them several months ago. Don't look fast and lean enough to make good cow ponies, do they? But Tom said he got them cheap. The man's a sucker for a bargain horse."

They said their good-byes. Halfway to the highway, Jane said with a frown, "I wonder why Tom bought those horses. They look like packhorses. He doesn't need them."

"Yes, he does," Santiago said quietly. "On weekends."

When Jane understood the implication of Santiago's words, she slammed on the brake to stop the truck. She turned and faced him. "Are you saying those are the packhorses you saw on the mesa? The ones used to carry smuggled goods?"

"Yes."

"How can you be so sure? It was dark, wasn't it?"

"There was a full moon. And one of the horses had that distinctive white blaze that the chestnut back there has. I'm sure those are the horses."

"That can't be! Tom can't be a smuggler. He goes to church, pays his taxes, and works part-time at the hardware store. . . ." Jane's voice trailed off.

"What?"

"Why would the hardware store hire him?" she asked, her expression puzzled. "The last time I was in the store, I talked to Bart Boyd and his son. He said he'd had to let his longtime helper go because there wasn't enough business."

"Bart Boyd," Santiago said, as if memorizing the name. "What's the son's name?"

"Jerry." Jane shook her head. "The Boyds can't be in on the smuggling either."

"Why not? *Querida,* when enough money is involved, anyone can be tempted."

Jane slumped against the steering wheel. "I can't believe

this. Especially about Tom. Penny would never go along with smuggling drugs and arms."

"She probably doesn't know," Santiago said gently. "It's not the sort of thing a man tells his wife, especially if he suspects she wouldn't approve of it."

Jane looked at Santiago, silently admitting that he might be right. With a heavy heart, she put the truck into gear and drove on.

At the four-way stop sign, Tom pulled up from the opposite direction. They exchanged greetings. After they drove on, she looked at Santiago.

"Was that the man you saw with the packhorses?"

"I can't be sure. Unlike his horse, Tom doesn't have a distinguishing mark. Except the voice. Both the men I saw had high, reedy voices. It could have been him."

Jane shuddered, thinking of what it was going to be like for Penny when she learned the truth.

As if to make up for spending the greater part of the day getting married, Jane worked like a demon. She ironed the checked tablecloths and napkins Susan liked to use. She mopped all the floors in the house and dusted the furniture, just in case one of the guests came inside.

After adding the vegetables to the meat in the casserole, she looked out the window from time to time to watch Santiago exercise the horses. *Her husband.* The words produced a flicker of excitement as well as a stab of anxiety. What had she done? Had she been out of her mind to marry this stranger? What did she really know about him?

Very little, and those scant facts she'd dragged out of him with difficulty. Now that they were married, maybe he'd share a little more of himself with her. Surely he would.

The intimacy of marriage . . . except there wouldn't be any intimacy. No pillow talk. No confiding of small secrets, fears, and hopes. She was doing it again. Anticipating and worrying about things. She had to stop that.

Jane fed and bathed the baby. After checking to see how

many horses Santiago had left to exercise, she decided to put Marisa to bed. The baby couldn't stay up that long yet. Once the baby was asleep, Jane changed clothes and went out to help Santiago.

"Do I have time to take a shower?" Santiago asked. "I reek of horses."

Jane didn't tell him that she rather liked the smell of horses. She forked a chunk of meat in the casserole before she answered. "You have ten minutes. After that, I can't guarantee the quality of our supper."

"I only need five," he said, unbuttoning his shirt and shrugging out of it on the way to the bathroom.

Jane watched him. Though they shared a house, she had never seen him in bright light without his shirt. She suddenly had to fan herself.

This was ridiculous. She'd endured a hot day without fanning herself, but one look at Santiago's broad shoulders and she felt hot and breathless. If only the evening were over—the evening of her wedding day. Then they could go on as before. As if nothing had happened.

Jane forced her attention back to the food. She took the green salad from the fridge and set the bowl on the table. For a moment she was tempted to cover the table with a cloth. She shook her head. What was the matter with her? She'd always used place mats. To do something fancier might suggest that she wanted this meal to be special. Even though it was her wedding day, under the circumstances it was better to handle it as any other day on the ranch.

By the time Santiago joined her, the food was ready.

They spoke casually of the weekend ahead and Susan Baldwin's camping party.

"Do you mind if I go along again?" he asked.

"Yes, I mind. I think it's too dangerous. What if they become suspicious?"

"They won't. To them I'm just another wetback of no particular consequence."

"You're wrong. You don't look meek enough to be of no consequence."

"What are you saying, *querida?* I look too—"

"Dangerous."

Santiago grinned.

"Anyone with any sense will recognize that you're not a man to tangle with unnecessarily," she said.

"The operative words are *with any sense*. I don't think those wranglers are blessed with great intelligence or common sense—or they wouldn't be doing what they're doing."

"But they are dangerous. Remember how they shot at me when I only wanted to ask if they'd seen any horses?"

"Another demonstration of their lack of sense."

"Using your argument that anyone can be seduced or bought if the money and the circumstances are right, will these same people not do almost anything to hang on to this money?"

"Good point," Santiago acknowledged. "But trust me on this. They won't see me as a threat. They're programmed by their prejudice to see someone who's inferior to them. By the time they recognize their mistake, it'll be too late."

"You've done this before, haven't you?" Jane asked. "Posed as a harmless peasant? A wolf in sheep's clothing?"

Santiago shrugged. "This is excellent stew."

"You're changing the subject. Don't think I'll always let you get away with that, but it's late, and it's been an eventful day." She rose and fetched the lemon bars. "Dessert."

"It looks delicious. I also have something." Santiago went to the fridge and removed a bottle from the vegetable bin.

"Champagne?" she asked.

"Sparkling white wine. I didn't recognize any of the Champagne brands at the supermarket, so I thought it would be safer to get the sparkling wine."

Jane fetched two wineglasses.

Santiago filled their glasses. "To what shall we drink?"

"How about that this isn't the biggest mistake we've ever made? That the next three years won't be a nightmare?"

"They won't be," Santiago said confidently. "A toast has to

be positive." He thought for a moment before he raised his glass. "To our future: may it be filled with happiness, harmony, and prosperity."

That certainly was positive, optimistic, and something to wish for, Jane reflected as she raised her glass.

"Speaking of prosperity," Santiago said, reaching for the jacket he had draped over a kitchen chair. He removed an envelope and handed it to Jane.

"What's this?" she asked.

"Something I promised you."

Jane skimmed the letter. She felt warmth rush to her face. Then relief washed over her so strongly that if she hadn't been sitting, her knees might have buckled.

"My bank loan," she whispered. "Marked *paid*."

"You look surprised. Didn't you believe I would keep my promise?"

"I believed you. It's just that seeing this . . ." She shook her head, unable to speak for a moment. "It's overwhelming. I feel like the proverbial ton of bricks has been lifted from my chest. Now no one can take my home from me. Thank you."

"I am glad I could do this, *querida*. It's little enough in exchange for what you have given me."

"Such as?"

"A home. Loving arms for Marisa. A chance to begin a new life." Santiago lifted one of her hands and kissed it. "Thank you," he murmured before he rushed from the room, overcome with emotion.

Jane watched her new husband walk out of the kitchen. Some of the tension drained out of her. She hadn't realized how tense she'd been, not knowing how this evening would end. Santiago had hit just the right note: a mixture of sentiment and reticence. They weren't ready for anything more intimate. Then why did she feel just a tiny bit disappointed?

Chapter Ten

As soon as the caravan stopped in the yard on Friday, Susan Baldwin hurried toward Jane.

"I heard you got married to your sexy hired hand. Can't blame you," Susan said, looking at Santiago working with the horses. "Congratulations."

"Thank you," Jane murmured, not liking the way the woman looked at Santiago—as if he were a prime steak ready to be devoured. Would Susan flirt with Santiago again, and, more to the point, how would she, Jane, react? Jane's first impulse was to grab those peroxided curls and give a good yank.

Be civil if it kills you. Jane clamped her teeth together to keep from speaking. Besides, it was up to Santiago to repulse Susan's flirtation. At least Jane hoped he would.

"I'd better help Leanne with lunch. Excuse me." Jane forced herself to smile at Susan before she walked away.

"Congratulations," Leanne said, when Jane joined her at the grill.

"How did you find out about us getting married?" Jane asked, curious and a little exasperated.

"You forget that we live in a sparsely populated area, so if anything happens to any of us, it's news to be shared. If one of us buys a new truck, it's all over the county in hours, so you can imagine how fast news of your wedding made the rounds."

Jane groaned. Then she shrugged, resigned. "I suppose it's a relief to folks to talk about something other than low beef prices and the lack of rain."

"That's for sure." Leanne chuckled. "Now that you're married, the crew at the seed and feed store won't have the widow of Windy Hill Ranch to speculate about."

"Is that what they called me?" Jane asked in disbelief.

"Or Owen Wilkerson's little girl."

"Oh, great. A widow or a girl," Jane muttered. "Why not a woman in her prime, which is what I am?" The women exchanged a look before they burst into laughter.

"Men can be such jerks," Leanne said. "You want to give the baked beans a stir?"

"Sure."

"I brought you a copy of the newspaper that has the announcement of your marriage in it. Right above the divorces granted and the notices of bankruptcies. I thought you might want to see it."

"Thanks." Jane had forgotten that the county paper listed court proceedings. It would spare her having to tell people.

When lunch was served, Jane walked to the front porch, where Santiago waited for her. "I brought you some food. You'd better eat." They sat side by side in the porch swing while he ate. "You haven't changed your mind about going with the campers?"

"I have to. There are still details I need to know."

Jane didn't bother to ask him what the details were, being pretty sure he wouldn't or couldn't tell her. "You be careful," she murmured, her voice raw and whispery with emotion. Thankfully, Santiago didn't seem to notice. Or if he did, he was kind enough not to comment on it. Jane, who was usually in control of her feelings, hated the fact that she suddenly found herself dangerously close to being a weepy woman. What was wrong with her?

"I'll be careful," Santiago said. "I promise." He turned and kissed her.

The sweet, gentle kiss ran all over her. "What was that for?" she murmured.

"In my country husbands kiss their wives before they

go on a trip." He smiled and added, "Besides, we have an audience."

Jane glanced at the campers, who were getting ready to leave. She caught both Susan and Leanne looking in the direction of the porch. "I'd forgotten about them."

"Will you be okay by yourself?" Santiago asked, his eyes filled with concern.

"Sure. I've lived here alone for quite some time, but thanks for asking." She was touched by his question, even if it was prompted only by politeness. Except Santiago didn't strike her as a man who did things merely to be polite. He seemed genuinely concerned. She risked a quick look at him, and her heart skipped a beat. His tawny eyes looked at her with a warmth that took her breath away.

"I'd better go," he murmured, and he rose.

She nodded and took the plate from him. She stood on the porch until she could no longer see the dust raised by the trucks. With a sigh, she turned to look at the debris of the luncheon. It would take her most of the afternoon to clean up.

Jane waited until Marisa woke from her nap before she started. The baby watched from the playpen Jane had set up in the shade of the tent. As long as Jane talked to her or sang, the baby was content.

It wasn't until well after dark that Jane had a chance to read the newspaper Leanne had brought her. She read the two lines that listed the bare facts of her marriage. There it was in black-and-white for all the world to see. For better or worse, she was really and truly married.

Jane turned her attention to the front page and the banner headline announcing a murder. She looked at the photo of the murder victim and gasped. She looked again. There was no mistake: it was the vendor from whom she had bought the locket. The locket that had belonged to Santiago's sister. What a bizarre coincidence.

Reading the article, she found out that the police had no suspects. Sheriff Ryback was quoted as saying that the fatal stabbing appeared to be the result of a robbery gone wrong.

That night, Jane double-checked all doors and windows to be sure they were locked.

On Saturday morning, a new and barely dusty pickup stopped in the yard. The driver approached the porch. Not recognizing him or the vehicle, Jane remained standing behind the locked screen door.

"Good morning. What can I do for you?" she called out, wanting him to stop at the bottom of the porch steps. He did.

"Good morning," the man replied, raising two fingers to the brim of his hat.

He made a sort of bobbing move with his head that reminded Jane of a turtle. She wished he'd remove his hat so she could see his face more clearly, but he didn't. What she saw of it showed a thin-lipped mouth, a square chin, and a bladelike nose. She waited for him to state his business.

"I'm looking for a man. His name is Gregorio Alvarado."

After the tiniest of pauses, which she hoped he hadn't noticed, Jane said, "Sorry, but I don't know anyone by that name." She was lying. Her new husband had signed the marriage license as Gregorio Santiago Alvarado.

"Really? I was told you had a hired hand who fit the description of Gregorio."

The man didn't entirely believe her and didn't try to hide his skepticism. Remembering what Santiago had told her about all foreigners looking alike to most people, she said, "Drifters look more or less alike, if you know what I mean." She shrugged. Then with a frown she asked, "What did you say your name was?" He hesitated just a beat, unwittingly revealing to Jane that he was going to lie. His head bobbed again like a turtle's. A nervous habit?

"I'm Jack Montgomery. I was told in town you had a hired hand."

"Before I got married I had a hired hand. Actually, several of them," Jane said, hoping she sounded both convincing and dismissing.

"What can you tell me about the most recent hired hand?"

From his voice, Jane concluded that he was trying to control his irritation and impatience. She lifted her shoulders in an elaborate shrug. "Nothing, really. As I said, drifters look sort of alike. They come and go. Why are you looking for this man?"

"Any idea where he went?"

He hadn't answered her question. She was done being interrogated. "He mentioned knowing some people in Dallas," Jane improvised, hoping the stranger would hightail it to east Texas. "Excuse me, but I have something in the oven."

Jane closed the heavy front door, which locked automatically. Thank heaven Santiago had insisted on installing a new, strong lock. Quickly she took the shotgun from the hall closet and inched her way next to the front window that overlooked the yard.

Knowing the man couldn't see her behind the semisheer curtains, she watched him. He was in no hurry to leave. He glanced around as if memorizing the layout of the ranch. She didn't like that. She didn't like him. He was, she suspected, one of those people who lied whether they had to or not. A liar. A user. A destroyer. A dangerous man.

She stood motionless, holding the gun securely, ready to use it if she had to. Finally he got into his truck and drove off. Quickly she opened the front door a crack and listened to the sound of the truck to be sure he actually left. She stood there until the noise of the engine had faded.

For the rest of the day she felt nervous and uneasy. Finally, she took her great-grandfather's gun belt from the wooden chest and strapped it around her waist. She placed the cleaned and loaded Colt into the holster.

That night, worrying about Santiago and what was happening on the mesa, Jane couldn't sleep. She took the shotgun from the closet, unlocked the door, and stepped out onto the front porch. She looked toward the mesa. It was almost midnight, so if a plane was going to land that night, it would happen soon.

Less than five minutes later a plane landed and, as before, left fifteen minutes later. What had it loaded or unloaded? Jane sat in the porch swing, worrying and wondering. The rhythmic swaying soothed her a little, until the sound of another engine interrupted the peaceful night.

"What on earth?" she muttered, and she rushed to the end of the porch. A second plane? What was going on? Soon the mesa would be as busy as the Dallas–Fort Worth airport. As she thought of the quantity of contraband being delivered to her range, red-hot rage surged through her.

On Sunday morning, she heard the sound of a car coming to a stop in the yard.

"Now who?" she muttered. Sometimes she didn't have a single visitor in two weeks, and now she had two in two days. Glancing out the window, she saw Deputy Wilson getting out of his squad car. *Great.* Jane stepped out onto the front porch.

"Hey, Bud. What are you doing so far from town?"

"I was out this way and thought I'd stop by. Heard you got married to your hired hand."

"Yes, I did. Did you stop to wish me well?" Her question obviously caught him off guard.

"I reckon, since it's a done deal," he acknowledged grudgingly.

"Thank you, Bud. I appreciate that."

Bud fiddled with his sunglasses as if what he was about to say was difficult.

"Why don't you just spit it out, Bud?"

"Okay, then. Did you marry Santiago so he can get a green card? If you did, I have to warn you that you could be in trouble. I told you before that the INS is cracking down on these fake marriages. Mrs. Winter will make a surprise visit, and she's no fool. She can smell a sham marriage a mile off."

With more confidence than she felt, Jane said, "Let her come. We have nothing to hide."

"For your sake, I hope so." Bud glanced around. "So, where's your new husband?"

"Leanne needed him to help her with the camping party."

"Well, at least he's a hard worker."

"He's a very hard worker," Jane added emphatically. She debated whether she should ask him about her visitor. She couldn't think of a reason she shouldn't. "Say, Bud, do you know a man named Jack Montgomery?"

"No. Why?"

"He came to the ranch yesterday. Something about him bothered me. The way he looked around."

"I'll run his name through the computer. You got your shotgun handy?"

"Yes."

"I know you're a good shot, but I still don't like the idea of you being here alone."

"Santiago will be back this afternoon." Jane paused for a moment, but then her curiosity got the better of her. "Leanne brought me a newspaper. I read about the murder. I bought something from the murdered man's booth on the Fourth. Any idea why he was stabbed?"

"Robbery. Leastwise, that's what the sheriff thinks."

"But you don't?"

"I suspect the vendor was involved in smuggling illegals."

"What makes you think that?"

"Jane, I can't tell you that. I'm still investigating. You keep that shotgun handy."

Over a late supper of scrambled eggs and ham on Sunday night, Jane studied Santiago's face but could not guess from his expression whether his mission had been successful or not. "Nobody grew suspicious of you?" she finally asked.

"I told you they wouldn't."

"Did you find out what you needed to know?"

"Yes."

Santiago didn't elaborate. She hadn't expected him to. She watched him surreptitiously, hungrily. She had missed him. He had been gone only forty-eight hours, but it had felt like forever. She had known him only a month or so, but that too seemed like forever. How could that be? She was no romantic girl whose head was filled with rosy, cozy illusions about relationships and love.

"Is there more iced tea?" Santiago asked.

"Of course." Glad to be roused from her introspective thoughts, Jane refilled his glass.

"I heard two planes land on the mesa last night."

"You stayed up?"

"I couldn't sleep, so I sat on the porch."

"This time the planes brought *in* two loads."

"Of what? Please don't tell me it's better that I don't know." Santiago remained silent for so long that Jane wasn't sure he'd answer. "I deserve to know what's happening on my land."

He looked at her silently. Then he nodded. "This time it was bales of marijuana."

Jane sighed. "I hate to speculate just how much pot two planes can hold."

"A small fortune's worth."

"And we're letting this poison into the country?"

"No."

"Good. But how are we keeping it from being picked up?"

"I've made arrangements. Don't worry," Santiago said.

"You mean, don't ask, don't you?"

"That too. The amount of pot we're talking about is worth a king's ransom. When these bales disappear, the drug lords will be very, very angry. They'll do anything to recover their merchandise. They torture people to get information. That's why I don't want you to know the details. I don't want to run the risk of you being tortured."

Jane shuddered. "Why don't we just call in the DEA and let them handle it?"

"Because I don't know whom I can trust," Santiago said. "Did anything else happen while I was gone?"

Jane pushed the newspaper toward him. "Do you recognize this man?"

Santiago glanced at the paper, then at her. "The vendor," he said with a frown. He read the article.

"Deputy Wilson came by this morning. He doesn't believe that the motive was a robbery gone wrong. He thinks the man was involved in smuggling illegals."

"The deputy could be right."

Santiago looked as if he were working something out in his mind. "I had another visitor," Jane said, and she told him about Jack Montgomery. There was no obvious physical reaction until she mentioned Montgomery's habit of moving his head like a turtle. Then Jane sensed a sudden tension in Santiago. "Did I handle this right? If the man is a friend, and if that is his real name—"

"He's no friend, and his real name is not Jack Montgomery. You did just fine."

It hit her then that Santiago wasn't surprised by the man's visit. "You expected him, didn't you?"

"Not him necessarily, but I thought someone would come around to ask questions. I didn't expect him so soon, though. That changes things."

"What things?"

Santiago shook his head. "The less you know, the better."

"I don't believe that. Ignorance is never better."

"It is in this case." Santiago's mouth tightened. "I am not leaving the ranch again. I will be around to handle whatever comes up."

"Why don't you tell me everything about this Jack Montgomery?"

"Not right now."

"Does that mean at some point you'll tell me everything about your life?"

Santiago considered that for a moment. "That'll depend on how things work out. Now please excuse me. I have to ride out and check on something on the range."

Jane clamped her teeth together to keep from telling him what she thought of men just then. When he reached the door, she said, "I'm no damsel in distress. I can handle just about anything."

He turned to look at her. "I know you can. That's what I admire most about you."

The next morning, while they worked side by side in the stable, Jane said, "You didn't get back to the house until after midnight. Why didn't you sleep longer this morning?"

Santiago regarded her with a raised eyebrow. "You think I'm so old and infirm that I can't do a full day's work after a short night?"

Jane couldn't prevent her gaze from raking over his wide shoulders, his trim waist, his strong, long legs. "Definitely not old and infirm," she said with a smile. To change the subject she said, "I forgot to tell you that when Deputy Wilson came by, I mentioned Jack Montgomery's visit. Bud said he'd run the name through the computer. Will that create problems?"

"No, and the deputy won't find anything on Jack Montgomery. At least not on the man who is using that name."

"Bud also warned me that Mrs. Winter from the INS will probably arrive one day to check up on us. That's the woman who was mentioned in that newspaper article I read to you before we were married, remember? Anyway, Bud didn't think that she'd be fooled easily about a fake marriage."

Santiago laid a hand on Jane's shoulder in a gesture of reassurance and felt her startled response. "That won't do, *querida*. Mrs. Winter would have to be blind, deaf, and dumb to miss that reaction. You can't jump back like that when I touch you."

Jane felt her face grow hot. "You caught me by surprise. I guess I've lived alone so long that I'm no longer used to being touched."

"We'll have to remedy that."

"What do you have in mind?" she asked, her throat tight.

"Just a little touching practice so that you don't shy away like a frightened filly. Come closer," he urged, his voice soft, seductive.

When she did, Santiago ran his hands up and down her bare arms, his touch gentle but firm, the work-hardened roughness of his fingers rasping against her skin, evoking a curiously pleasurable sensation. Jane kept her eyes lowered, not daring to look at him, afraid he might guess how much she liked his touch.

"Then I might also touch you like this," he said, running his hands over her back, down to her waist. "You are so tense," he murmured. "Relax."

How could she relax, when his nearness, his touch, interfered with her thinking, her breathing?

"You have to touch me too," he said. "Mrs. Winter will not be convinced if the caressing is one-sided. Do it, *querida*," Santiago urged.

She nodded, her mouth too dry to speak. She trailed her fingers over his chest, feeling the softness of the cotton shirt he wore.

"Yes, like that," he murmured encouragingly.

He had left the two top buttons on his shirt undone. Her fingertips touched the warm skin, the coarse-silk dark curls on his chest. She heard him suck in his breath.

"You're too tense. Relax," she said, echoing his words.

Santiago chuckled. He caught her hands in his. "Enough touching for now, or the horses will not get fed today."

"Right," Jane said, mostly glad that he'd ended the sweet torture.

Chapter Eleven

When Jane arrived at the county road to get their mail, she was surprised to find three big boxes piled around the mailbox.

"Look, Marisa, packages," she said to the baby, who gurgled happily in her car seat. "But none of these are for us."

Jane examined the postmarks. Maryland. Like the earlier packages Santiago had received. Lifting them onto the truck, she was astounded at their weight. All the way to the ranch, she speculated about their contents.

From his expression, Santiago had obviously been expecting them. He carried them into the tack room.

"Aren't you going to open them to see what's in them?" Jane asked.

"I know what's in them. Things to make the ranch more secure."

"A security system?" Jane asked with a frown. "That doesn't make any sense. We're too far from town—"

"Not a security system exactly. More like a warning system that announces visitors before they get too close."

Jane struggled with that information for a bit. "So that we can prepare for their arrival?"

"Exactly."

"And how do we do that? The shotgun, the Colt—"

"If necessary. I'll show you what I received later. I want to install these safety measures before it gets dark."

"Can I help?"

"No, thanks."

* * *

Four hours later Santiago called her. Jane, with Marisa on her hip, joined him outside.

"I've set up a trip wire around the perimeter of the buildings and sensors on the road leading to the ranch from the highway and from the mesa."

Jane stared at Santiago, wide-eyed. She had to moisten her lips before she could speak. "How will we know the wire's been tripped or that the sensors picked up something?"

"We'll hear the signal in the house. The outer sensors and wires will give us a six-minute warning and the ones close to the buildings two minutes."

"Two minutes?" Jane asked, her voice faint.

"Long enough to grab a weapon. I've also buried explosives in the yard that can be set off by a well-aimed bullet." Jane blinked while she processed that information. Santiago hated to have to tell her these things.

"I feel like I'm living in a frontier fort," she murmured.

"These are just precautionary measures," he assured her. "If everything goes according to plan, nothing will happen at the ranch. You and Marisa will be safe."

"So all this is in case your plan doesn't work?"

"Yes. A fallback position. Insurance, if you will. I want to be sure that you and Marisa have some protection, just in case. But I'm confident that we will not need any of these."

When Jane didn't say anything, Santiago asked, "Is dinner almost ready? I'm hungry." He *was* hungry, but he asked about food mainly to distract her. She was too pale, too stunned.

Jane nodded. "We can eat as soon as you come inside."

Santiago watched her walk into the house. Silently he cursed his former comrade. If not for his betrayal, none of this would be necessary. He had watched Jane closely. He had not missed the fear she had tried to hide. Something else to be added to his ex-partner's list of sins—and to his own.

A woman like Jane shouldn't be exposed to the brutality, the horror of the war that raged around the billion-dollar business of drugs and arms. No woman should. Yet for her own safety, her survival, he'd had to tell her. He would do everything in his power to meet his betrayer far from the house.

Santiago joined Jane in the kitchen. He took the M-16 with him. He laid it on the kitchen counter.

Jane's eyes became saucerlike when she saw the weapon. Then she stared at it for a good thirty seconds. "Are you going to teach me how to shoot this . . . whatever it is?"

"An M-16. I think you'll do better with the weapons you're used to."

Jane flicked another look at the weapon.

"You have your shotgun and your Colt." Removing a handgun from the soft cloth in which it had been wrapped, he said, "And here's a .38 and four clips." He laid the pistol and the clips on the counter. "Where do you want to keep it?"

Jane took an empty cookie can from the shelf. "Will this do? I doubt anyone would expect to find a gun in a cookie tin."

"The tin will do." He picked up the gun. "All you have to do is click the safety off, aim, and shoot. Very simple."

Jane picked up the pistol to get the feel of the gun. She nodded her approval before she placed everything in the tin. Then she covered it with a clean cloth napkin and poured the contents of a box of crackers on top. She was about to put it back into the cupboard but changed her mind. She set it next to the ceramic canisters holding flour and sugar. "In case I need it in a hurry," she said to Santiago.

He nodded. He showed her where he had buried the explosives. Each little mound could be hit from one of the windows in the house. "I know from seeing you shoot on the mesa that you are good enough to hit the explosives with your first bullet. That should keep anyone from rushing the house."

Jane grew even paler. She moistened her lips but didn't say anything. To Santiago, the gravity of her expression intensified the solemn beauty of her face, and he felt his chest tighten. "I am so sorry, *querida,* that I had to put fear into your beautiful eyes. I would give anything to make it go away."

"It's not your fault. You didn't cause these people to use

my land as their smuggling route. If it's anyone's fault, it's mine. I—"

"You let them use your land for camping. That's all. You're not responsible for their criminal activities."

"I'd feel better if we told the sheriff or somebody in state or Federal law enforcement."

Her eyes pleaded with him. Santiago looked away. "We will. As soon as I know whom we can trust." He felt her studying him and wondered how much she trusted *him*. He had done nothing yet to earn her trust. "I know it looks as if I am inviting trouble to the ranch, but I'm not. I have only installed some simple defensive measures. Just in case."

She nodded.

Santiago wished she would say something. Not just anything, but something that would not make him feel so guilty. With a start he realized he wanted absolution, and that was a lot to ask for.

He knew he could call the DEA to intercept the next shipment of drugs. He also knew that he could contact the director of the Omega Group, who would send men to help him, but there might be a leak. Or he could alert the media, whose watchful presence would lead to an investigation that would, in turn, result in the arrest of most of the smugglers but probably not all. And he wanted *all* of them caught. Especially the head honcho, the one who had betrayed him. Nothing less was acceptable—not even if it caused fear and concern for the one woman who had touched his heart as no other had in a long, long time.

A part of him hated that he felt like that, that he personally wanted to mete out justice, but thinking of Corazon, of all the members of his family who had died, he subdued that small voice. He knew what he had to do. The blood of the dead cried out for justice and retribution.

Another heat wave settled over the area. Even Jane, who was used to hot summers, felt her energy flagging. When Santiago announced after lunch that he wanted to work on the south fence, Jane put her foot down.

"Not in this heat. At least not in the middle of the day. I'd end up having to go out looking for you come sundown."

He raised an eyebrow. "You think I might collapse?"

"Heatstroke is more common—and more dangerous—than you think. It's common sense to do the chores around the ranch that can be done in the shade."

Santiago had to concede that what Jane said made sense. He started to clear the table.

"I didn't mean to hint that you had to help in the house."

"I know, but why not? I noticed that you have set up the ironing board. Though I have never ironed, I have washed dishes. If you don't trust me to get them clean, you can inspect them afterward," he said with a grin.

That grin caused the butterflies that had taken up residence in Jane's stomach since Santiago's arrival to flutter to life. Nor could she look at that smile without smiling back. "I expect you to wash the back of the plates too."

"I would not dream of not washing the back," he replied solemnly, but another smile pulled at the corners of his mouth. He could not remember if he had actually ever washed an eating utensil in anything but a creek, pond, or rain puddle. If the men he had served with in the jungles and the mountains could see him squirting pink detergent into a sink, they would laugh their heads off.

He had no desire to go back to that kind of life. Now he had a place where he was beginning to feel at home, to belong, with a set routine, specific tasks, none of which included shooting at human beings or being shot at. There was much to be said for that. And for the fact that he slept on ironed sheets, and without cradling a weapon. Now if only his arms could cradle the soft-spoken woman who moved gracefully through the kitchen, he would feel as if he had found paradise on earth.

Don't dream. Don't hope. At least not yet. Too often he had seen a comrade start to fantasize about those things, become careless, and get killed. His fight was not over yet. His biggest personal fight was ahead of him. He could not afford to become careless. If he did, he might not survive. That thought did not terrify him nearly as much as the knowledge that if he did not survive, neither would Marisa or Jane—and that was unthinkable.

Jane woke up, her senses alert. She had lived alone long enough to become alert instantly at unusual noises. It wasn't the baby fussing. It wasn't the horses being spooked by something. Quietly, she removed the Colt and the gun belt holding the extra ammunition from the nightstand before she padded barefoot into the hall. She sensed Santiago before she saw him standing beside the window next to the front door.

"You heard something too?" she whispered.

"The sensors went off."

Jane shivered. "Someone is close to the buildings."

"Yes."

Jane peered out into the darkness. At first she saw nothing out of the ordinary. Then a movement near the corral gate caught her eye. The shape of a human figure. By the size of it, a man. When he turned toward the house, she gasped.

Santiago's hand shot out and covered her mouth. "He is wearing night-vision goggles," he whispered.

Jane nodded, her heart racing. When Santiago removed his hand, she murmured, "For a second I thought he was the man from outer space my cowhands saw on the mesa."

"Easy," Santiago murmured soothingly. His hand rested on her shoulder. "Let's see what they're up to."

"They?"

"There's another one by the tack room."

"I see him. Any more?"

"One more. By the stable."

"Are they after the horses?"

"I doubt it."

"What, then?" She looked at him, his face a pale shape in the darkness. When Santiago didn't answer her, Jane turned her gaze back to the yard. "I'm not letting them take the horses."

"Neither am I," he assured her.

They watched the man emerge from the stable. He paused until the other two joined him. They appeared to hold a short conference before they turned and faced the house. Jane shuddered. The night-vision goggles gave the men an eerie, otherworldly, menacing air. Santiago raised the M-16.

"Cover the other window," he whispered, "but don't shoot unless I do. No matter what happens, hold your fire. Jane, do you hear me?"

"Yes. I won't shoot until you do," she repeated, her mouth so dry, she could barely whisper the words. She took her position by the other window. In movies they always knocked out the glass before they shot out of a window. That would make a tremendous racket in the night's stillness and betray their positions.

"What on earth are they talking about for so long?" she asked.

"It has been only a minute or so."

He was undoubtedly right, but it seemed like an hour to Jane. She raised her arm to wipe the sweat from her forehead. When the men started to move, she quickly assumed the classic shooter's stance, knees bent, both hands on the gun.

She wished she had grabbed the shotgun from the hall closet. Not that this was going to be the showdown at the O.K. Corral. It would be over fast, one way or the other. Most likely in their favor. They had the thick stone walls of the house as cover, and Santiago's M-16 could spew out bullets faster than the eye could blink. And what she lacked in firepower, she made up for in accuracy. Annie Oakley had nothing on her.

"Easy, Jane," Santiago said, his voice a reassuring whisper. "They are not coming toward the house."

Jane closed her eyes for a moment, trying to clear them of the frightening images. Santiago was right. The men veered off toward the highway, but she didn't move until she heard the sound of a car driving away from the ranch.

"You can put the gun down," Santiago said.

She lowered the gun and let Santiago take it from her. He placed it on the floor next to the M-16 before he put his arms around her. And not a moment too soon. She trembled violently. Her knees threatened to buckle.

Santiago held her against him. He stroked her hair, murmuring soft words in Spanish. When her trembling subsided, he said, "It's all right. They are gone."

"But they'll be back, won't they?"

"Perhaps, but I doubt it."

"What were they looking for?"

Santiago knew exactly what the men had searched for, but it was safer for Jane not to know. "I think they just came to look. To reconnoiter." Gently he raised her face. He couldn't let her think about tonight's events too long. He had to downplay them.

"You did very well. Remained calm and—"

"Ha! I was scared to death the whole time. My heart was beating so loud, I was afraid they'd hear it."

"It's good to be afraid. Everybody is afraid. Or they ought to be. Otherwise they become careless."

"Were you afraid? You didn't look as if you were."

Santiago shrugged. "When you have been in the . . . danger business as long as I have, you learn to mask the signs of fear. But the fear is there. It makes you sharp, gives you an edge."

"I never knew that fear had a smell and a taste," Jane confessed. "I can't exactly describe the smell, except it's sort of acrid. Sharp enough that it hurts when you breathe it in."

"Not a bad description. And the taste?"

"Metallic on the tongue. Like chewing on aluminum foil."

Santiago knew she needed to talk, to let the adrenaline drain from her body. Men always found it necessary to talk after moments of danger, so why shouldn't a woman?

"Speaking of scent and taste," he murmured, wrapping a strand of her hair around one finger. "Your hair smells so good, like wildflowers and jasmine. So pleasant to a man's senses.

And so soft to the touch." He released the strand and tangled both hands in her long hair. He loved the chestnut color with the reddish highlights, the heaviness of it in his hands, the clean, silken texture, the sweet, sense-numbing smell when he buried his face in it.

"What makes you so sure those men won't be back? Maybe they went to get more men."

Santiago trailed soft kisses along her neck before he answered. "What would make them think they needed more men? I am sure they believe we slept through their visit and that they could have taken us without any trouble."

Jane shivered again. "Still—"

Santiago stopped her words with a quick kiss. "*Querida,* if they wanted to do us harm, they would have stormed the house. Or at least tried to. They would not have even reached the porch, but, of course, they would not have known that. They only came to look." He feathered kisses along her jawline. When his lips touched her throat, he inhaled the scent of her skin.

"What are you doing?" Jane asked, a little surprised.

"Ah, you finally noticed that I am trying to get your attention, man to woman."

"I noticed. Are you trying to distract me from what happened?"

"Am I succeeding?"

"Yes," she admitted. "I also had the impression that you were sniffing me. Do I smell?" she asked, alarmed.

"I should hope so! It would be tragic if you did not. Don't you know that smell is one of the most exciting senses we have?"

"Yes, but—"

"No buts. A world without smell would be a dreadful place, and a woman without an innate scent a tragedy worthy of Shakespeare."

"Right up there with *Romeo and Juliet?*"

"And *King Lear.*" He was succeeding in making her relax.

"What do I smell like?" she couldn't resist asking. "I didn't use any perfume, and I don't think my soap has a pronounced fragrance—"

"I was talking about the unique scent that would let me find you in the dark."

Jane hadn't known she possessed such a scent. Somewhat worried, she wondered what it was. What if her scent was unpleasant? With a start, she realized how turned off she was by a bad smell. Once, as a teenager, she'd let milk boil over, and it had taken years before she could bear to drink milk again without remembering that burned smell. What if Santiago hated how she smelled?

Jane was about to skid into a marathon session of worrying when Santiago bent down to kiss her throat. Surely he couldn't stand to kiss her if he hated her scent. "What do I smell like?"

Santiago kissed her throat, where her pulse beat satisfyingly fast, before he answered. "I have been trying to identify the scent, but it is elusive. Let me try again."

Jane felt his warm breath skitter over her skin like gossamer. She shivered, but this time not from fear. If he took much longer, she wouldn't be able to stop herself from moaning with frustration and desire.

Santiago murmured something, his lips close but not quite touching her.

"Mmm. Earthy. Satisfying."

"What is?"

"Your scent. Like freshly baked tortillas."

Jane felt as if hit by a bucket of cold water. "That's awful! Why couldn't I smell like a gardenia?"

"No, it's wonderful. Tortillas are life-sustaining. Fundamentally nourishing. Deeply sating and satisfying. What is a flower that turns brown at the first touch compared to that? Nothing. Less than nothing."

Put that way, the smell of tortillas didn't sound quite so pedestrian.

Santiago kissed her, stopping her worrying, her speculating, her thinking. The pent-up feelings of the past weeks flared into flame. How long they kissed and touched Jane couldn't have said. All she knew was that she felt faint yet so alive, insensate yet hungry for his touch. She must have moaned or called his name, for Santiago stopped as if turned to stone.

"Jane, stop, please." Santiago rubbed his forehead as if coming out of a trance. "I can't believe I told you to stop." His voice held a hint of dismay.

"But you did. Why?" she managed to ask, her voice labored.

"Because if you come to me now, it would be for the wrong reason. You would come because of what happened this evening."

"Because I'd been afraid?"

"Yes. Because death came near us. You felt his presence, you smelled his fetid breath. I know that once we have been in death's presence, we feel the overwhelming need for something life-affirming. There is nothing more life-affirming than love."

Jane had never thought about that, but there was truth in Santiago's assertion. A lot of truth. Where did that leave them?

"Jane, come to me when you are ready. When you want me for myself. Not as a comfort, a reassurance, because you have been afraid." Santiago kissed her on the cheek before he rushed out of the kitchen.

Raising her hands and pressing them against her forehead, she tried to quiet the tumult raging inside her. Jane staggered to the kitchen sink and turned on the faucet. She splashed cold water over her face, her shoulders. Her gown got wet and felt good against her heated skin.

When she heard the shower gush on in the bathroom, she smiled a little. She was ready to bet the ranch that Santiago's shower would be long and cold.

Chapter Twelve

If it hadn't been for the M-16 lying on the kitchen counter, Jane might have thought that the previous night's events had been a dark dream. Though no nightmare, the stealthy visit by the night-goggled figures had been every bit as menacing as any bad dream that had ever stalked her sleep.

She noted, gratefully, that Santiago had already made coffee. The squawked greeting from Paco's cage showed that he had also taken care of the bird. Had Santiago slept at all? As she filled her mug, she wondered where he was.

Even as her brain formulated the alarming thought that he had heard something and had gone out to investigate, she nearly dropped the coffeepot in her haste to sprint to her bedroom. She grabbed the Colt and gun belt. Stationing herself next to the same window they had used the night before, Jane studied the yard, the corral, the buildings. She could detect nothing that shouldn't be there. Nor did anything seem to be missing, except Santiago. Where was he?

Bone-deep anxiety fused her to the wall and kept her there for long minutes. She realized that eventually she would have to go outside to look for him. Jane swallowed hard when she discovered that she was not only anxious, but afraid.

Jane took deep breaths, but that was only a delaying tactic. She could wait no longer. She had to find Santiago. With unsteady hands, she strapped the gun belt around her waist and opened the front door. Crossing the yard with quick steps, she watched for any movement. When she reached the stable and the door opened, she jumped back with a cry of alarm.

"Jane, I didn't mean to frighten you," Santiago said, placing his arms around her to steady her.

"I didn't know where you were."

She allowed herself to lean against him. For a moment she experienced the same delight at touching him she had felt the night before. Then her fingers touched the shoulder holster and handgun he wore under the shirt he hadn't tucked in. Santiago had never walked around armed before. In a flash she perceived that after last night everything had changed.

"Are you all right?" he asked.

"Yes." Jane took a couple of steps back, breaking the physical contact with Santiago.

"I came to check to be sure that our midnight visitors had not left us a surprise," he said.

"You mean like a booby trap? I hadn't even considered that possibility."

"No reason you should have." Santiago glanced at her gun belt.

Suddenly self-conscious, she touched the big belt buckle. "I know I look ridiculous. Like some bandit queen from a low-budget Western, but—"

"You look prepared. And you look beautiful."

Jane felt her face grow warm. She looked away quickly. "Did they leave a surprise?"

"No. I didn't think they had, but I wanted to make sure. Jane, I have been meaning to ask, why don't you have a dog? Most ranches do. Dogs are a great natural deterrent to uninvited visitors."

"I used to have dogs, but after the last one died, I couldn't . . ." Her voice trailed off.

"You became attached to them, and losing them hurt too much," he said softly.

"I didn't know I was so transparent."

"You aren't, but you are a woman with a warm, caring heart and a great capacity for love, so it was not hard to guess why you didn't replace the dogs."

She had never heard herself described like that. Quickly she said, "I know I should get another dog. I've been meaning to before Father Anselmo dumps a basket of puppies on my doorstep. He's threatened to do that."

Santiago chuckled. "That sounds just like him."

"Doesn't it, though?" Jane turned toward the stable. "May as well get started."

After breakfast Santiago rode out to repair the south fence, promising to be back before noon. Jane took the playpen outside so Marisa could watch her as she hung up the loads of laundry she had done that morning.

She heard the phone ring. "I'll be right back, sweetie," she said to the baby before she ran into the house. She picked up the receiver after the fifth ring.

"Oh, it's you, Penny. I was outside, hanging up the wash."

"Your dryer costs only a few pennies a load—why don't you use it?"

"Sunshine kills all residual germs in the baby's diapers. Marisa's never had diaper rash," Jane said proudly.

"That's another thing I don't understand. Why don't you use disposable diapers the way everybody else does?"

"Because they're expensive, and because they aren't biodegradable. Bad for the land." Before Penny could voice another well-meaning criticism, Jane asked, "Is there something I can do for you, or did you call just to chat?"

"Somebody stopped by to ask directions to your place."

Visions of goggle-eyed men danced before Jane's eyes before she realized that they already knew how to get to her ranch.

"Is everything okay at your place?"

"Yes. Who asked for directions?"

"Some woman. There was a logo on the side of her car, like some government agencies have, but I wasn't wearing my glasses, so I couldn't see what it was."

Immigration? It had to be. Jane tried to remain calm as she asked, "How long ago was this woman at your place?"

"About five minutes. I wasn't sure it was important enough to call—"

"Thanks, Penny." Jane dropped the receiver into its cradle. She heard the six-minute warning signal go off.

She flew into Santiago's room and scooped up the clothes he kept in the top drawer of the dresser. In her bedroom she crammed his underwear into her lingerie drawer and stuffed his T-shirts next to her own. Jane's gaze swept through the room. She pulled the lingerie drawer out a bit so its contents could be seen.

Then she jerked the bedspread back and mussed the bedding to suggest that two people had slept in the bed. She grabbed the unused pillow and exchanged it for Santiago's. When she saw the carefully folded boxer shorts he apparently slept in, she took them and tossed them across the bed. As an extra touch, she took her nightgown from under her pillow and flung it across her bed. It landed next to the boxer shorts.

The two-minute warning bell nearly gave her a heart attack. She flew out the back door, rounded the house, and picked up a pair of wet jeans as the car came to a stop in the front yard.

"Hello, there," the woman getting out of the car called out.

"Hello," Jane said, noting the car's logo. Her hands shook as she finished hanging up Santiago's jeans. She took time to smooth the denim fabric to give herself a moment to collect her thoughts. Then she turned to face the woman whose high-heeled shoes made it necessary for her to pick her way gingerly across the uneven yard. An attractive woman with a self-confident, no-nonsense air, she took in Jane, the baby, and the laundry. This was not a woman who could be fooled easily.

"I'm Mrs. Winter from Immigration."

Jane had guessed as much. "How do you do?"

Coming straight to the point, Mrs. Winter said, "You recently married an immigrant. I'm here to check up on a few things. We do that with everybody," she said with a smile.

Was she trying to put Jane at ease? Lull her into carelessness with a few casual words?

"What would you like to know?" Jane asked.

"It's hot out here in the sun," Mrs. Winter said, glancing meaningfully toward the house.

"Why don't we go inside?" Jane said. She picked up Marisa.

"Your husband's baby?"

"His niece." Surely that fact appeared in the records.

"Oh, yes. Now I remember."

Jane led the way into the house. When Marisa fussed, she said, "Why don't we go into the kitchen? Marisa is thirsty, and I could use some iced tea. How about you?"

"Iced tea would be fine."

With a hand motion, Jane invited Mrs. Winter to sit at the table. After pouring and serving the tea, she sat down to give Marisa a bottle of apple juice.

"So, how are things going?"

"Fine. The heat wave makes us listless and a little cranky, but otherwise we're all right."

"Your husband is cranky?"

"No. I meant the baby and I get cranky. He's even-tempered, sweet, and caring."

Mrs. Winter's left eyebrow rose a little. "That's quite an endorsement."

"It's not an endorsement. It's the truth. Santiago is a fine man."

"And a fine *husband?*"

"Yes," Jane said emphatically, knowing she'd come close to blowing it. "He's a fine *man* and a fine *husband.* I don't think he could be one without being the other."

"Probably not. What sort of father is he to the baby?"

"He's a great father. He adores Marisa and she him."

"And you? How do you feel?"

"I adore Marisa too. And Santiago," she added softly. That was true, she discovered with a start. And she had admitted it out loud. Did the woman believe her? Jane couldn't tell.

"So, you intend to stick with him for the requisite three years?"

Stick with him? Was the woman trying to rile her, prod her into saying something incriminating? As calmly as she could, Jane said, "We said 'until death do us part.' I hope that's a lot longer than three years."

"Good answer. One of the best I've heard, and I've heard a lot of them in these sham-marriage situations."

Jane bit the inside of her cheek to keep from saying something nasty to this officious, offensive woman.

"Mrs. Winter, there is nothing I can say to you to convince you that this isn't a sham marriage—short of inviting you into our bedroom, which I'm not about to do."

"Oh, but you will. I need to see the rest of the house."

Having no choice, Jane rose too, and put the baby against her shoulder to burp her. Then she led the way out of the kitchen.

"This is the living room." She pointed to the door across from the kitchen. "The bedrooms are at the back of the house."

While Mrs. Winter inspected the baby's room, Jane had a chance to give her bedroom a quick once-over. She wished she'd had a chance to drape one of Santiago's shirts over the chair.

"Nice big rooms," Mrs. Winter remarked.

She looked at Jane's bed for a long time—or so it seemed to Jane, who held her breath. Had she succeeded in creating the illusion that a husband and wife occupied this room?

"That four-poster must be an heirloom," Mrs. Winter remarked. "I like antiques. If you ever want to sell the bed, give me a call. My family owns an antiques store." She handed Jane a business card. "I'll be back."

Jane followed her to the porch and watched her drive away. Then she returned to the bedroom and sank onto the bed with the baby. Lying side by side with Marisa, she breathed deeply, only now fully realizing how tense and anxious she'd been.

"You think we did all right?" she asked, letting Marisa play with her hair. Jane went over everything she'd said, everything Mrs. Winter had said, every gesture and every nuance. She couldn't be sure what Mrs. Winter really thought.

Noting that Marisa had fallen asleep, Jane closed her eyes, intending to rest for just a few minutes.

* * *

Jane felt something soft and warm touch her lips. Her eyes opened to look straight into Santiago's tawny eyes, mere inches from hers. He was lying next to her, his head bent over hers.

"What?" she murmured.

"I left two fully awake females here a couple of hours ago, only to return to find two sleeping beauties, one of whom I have to kiss awake."

His lips touched hers again, a little more firmly, sending warm, thrilling messages to each cell in her body. The man sure was a good kisser. And he was hers. Well, only legally, but that could change.

Jane hadn't gone to confession recently because she would have to confess a lot of wayward thoughts. And the fact that her marriage was a lie. Although she knew Father Anselmo would not betray a confession, she was too embarrassed even to whisper the truth about her unconsummated marriage in the dusky light of the confessional.

Spiritually she was on shaky ground. And legally? Had she managed to fool Mrs. Winter? Thinking of the Immigration official, Jane extricated herself from Santiago's embrace and sat up.

"Mrs. Winter came for a visit this morning."

"I'm sorry I wasn't here. How did it go?" he asked.

"I'm not sure. The six-minute warning gave me a chance to move some of your things into this room, but I don't know if that convinced her."

Santiago grinned at her. "I was wondering what my shorts were doing on your bed, snuggled up to your nightgown. Don't worry, *querida*. How is she going to prove that we're not sharing this bed? And by the time she comes again, who knows what will have happened?"

The look he gave her, suggesting that not only their pajamas would share the bed, caused Jane's pulse to quicken and her heart to pound. Not wanting Santiago to know how his words had affected her, she drew a shallow breath and said, "Why don't you rest until lunch is ready? You got even less sleep than me." With that she fled to the safety of the kitchen to prepare lunch.

Another package from Maryland arrived. Among other items, it contained two cell phones. Santiago seemed relieved and pleased to have them. After making Jane promise to phone if anything happened, he left to work on the north fence. Besides being one of the never-ending chores on a ranch, repairing fences was also physically hard work, work that demanded a hearty meal.

As Jane studied the contents of her freezer, the six-minute warning bell went off. *Drat.* Not knowing if the visitor was friend or foe, Jane leaned the shotgun next to the front door and tried to stick the Colt into the waistband of her jeans. The gun was too big. Quickly she took the .38 from the cookie tin and shoved it into the waistband. She pulled her T-shirt over it.

Muttering a few choice words, she ran to the bedroom, where she exchanged her T-shirt for a cotton blouse. The two-minute warning sent her sprinting to the front porch, from where she watched a pickup park at the old hitching rail. Jane relaxed when she recognized the truck as belonging to Leanne. But it wasn't her friend who got out of the truck.

Why was Leanne's assistant coming to the ranch? Byron had never come alone before but always as part of the camping crew. Remembering Santiago's suspicion that Leanne's assistants might be involved with the smuggling, Jane rested her right hand on her waist, mere inches from the .38.

"Hey, Miz Peterson," Byron said, approaching her. He stopped at the bottom of the porch steps.

Jane returned the greeting.

"We left one of our coolers at the campground last time we were up there," he said. "Leanne wants me to get it." He paused for a beat, not looking at Jane. "We're always short of coolers, and they ain't exactly cheap," he added, shuffling from one foot to the other. "Can I drive to the mesa to get it?"

"Sure," Jane said. "How's Leanne?"

"She's fine. Thank you, ma'am." Without another word, Byron hurried to the truck and drove off.

He certainly was eager to retrieve that cooler. Jane didn't remember ever hearing Leanne complain of being short of coolers. And he was driving way too fast for the unpaved road leading to the mesa. Jane shook her head.

Byron had always struck her as a little lazy. Now he was not only moving fast, but he must have gotten out of bed at the crack of dawn to get to the ranch before eight. She couldn't picture him as an early riser. With a frown, she watched the dust cloud raised by the speeding truck. Then she shrugged.

Yet she couldn't dismiss his uncharacteristic behavior. What if she followed him at a discreet distance? If he spotted her, she could claim she was checking on her cattle.

Quickly she strapped Marisa into the car seat. As always, the baby was delighted to be going for a ride. Jane ran back into the house for Santiago's binoculars.

Byron's truck was far enough ahead that she was certain he couldn't see the dust her truck raised. Every couple of miles or so, she stopped to locate the plume of his dust with the binoculars. An hour later she'd lost sight of the dust.

"Baby girl, we lost him. Did he stop or go off the trail?" Jane slowly swept the binoculars across the horizon. On her third sweep, she saw the dust cloud.

"What's he doing so far south of the campground? The missing cooler isn't there. If there ever was a missing cooler."

Jane drove faster, narrowing the distance between them slightly. When she checked the dust plume again, it was a mere wisp. Byron had stopped driving.

Jane pulled off the trail and parked the truck behind a boulder that shielded her from view. Sitting in the truck, she watched him searching for something. And it couldn't be for a cooler. The area was totally unsuited for camping. What was he looking for?

After fifteen minutes he gave up. Byron slapped his hat against his leg several times. Though she couldn't read his lips, she was sure he was cussing up a blue streak. In a final burst of frustration, he kicked the truck's front tire before he jumped into the driver's seat and gunned the engine.

Since she couldn't outrun him, she decided to stay put. He couldn't see her from the road. She waited ten minutes before she drove home, scolding herself for having wasted a good part of the morning.

She'd just put a pot of chili on to cook and mixed the ingredients for corn bread when the six-minute warning sounded.

"Now who?" she grumbled. She reached for the .38 again and positioned herself by the window to watch. Maybe she should start wearing the gun all the time.

Jane relaxed when the sheriff's car came into view. Shocked, she watched him drive past the house without glancing at it. To drive onto someone's land without so much as a by-your-leave was exceedingly rude. Sheriff Ryback wasn't a charmer, but ordinarily he wasn't downright ill-mannered either. What was going on? Was he also looking for something?

A few minutes later Santiago returned.

"I saw dust on the trail. Whose is it?"

"The sheriff's. I guess he must be searching for something too."

" 'Too'? Who else was here?"

"Byron. He said they'd forgotten a cooler, and he wanted permission to go get it, but he lied."

"How do you know that?"

"I followed him, and he wasn't looking for a cooler."

"You did what?"

"You don't have to shout at me," Jane protested, surprised. This was the first time Santiago had raised his voice to her. "I stayed way back. He didn't know I was watching him."

"You're sure of that? And what makes you think he isn't dangerous?"

"Byron?" she asked, her voice disbelieving.

"Just because he appears to be a lazy, self-centered lout doesn't mean he can't turn violent to protect something that he thinks is his. *Querida,* let me remind you: when lots of money is involved, greed can make almost anyone do almost any-thing." Santiago cradled her face with his hands. "Jane, prom-ise you won't ever do something like that again."

The force of his powerful presence, the intense tawny eyes, the low voice, made Jane go soft in the knees. But she couldn't abdicate all responsibility for what happened on her land.

"I can't make such a promise, and you know it. I'm not into blind obedience and voiceless submission."

Santiago couldn't help but smile a little at the words she had chosen. "No, you aren't, and I'm not asking for 'blind obedi-ence and voiceless submission.' I dislike those qualities. I want an intelligent, full-blooded woman, not a dishrag. But I do want you to be more careful. I don't want anything bad to hap-pen to you. I'm sorry I raised my voice to you." He kissed her gently on the lips before he released her.

"And weren't you supposed to use your cell phone to call me if anything happened?" he demanded.

"Yes, but I thought you meant anything suspicious."

"You believed the story about the cooler?"

"No, not really," she admitted reluctantly. "But what are they looking for? There's nothing up there except—" Her voice broke off as she studied his face. "You know what they're look-ing for and where it is, don't you?"

"*Querida,* as far as you're concerned, there is nothing up there except the usual assortment of scorpions—"

"I hate being kept in the dark!"

"I know," Santiago said, his voice soothing. "But Byron ob-viously believed that you knew nothing, and so did the sheriff. That's good, because as long as everyone thinks that, they won't try to make you talk."

Jane wondered how long she could hold out under torture before she told them everything she knew. Not long, she suspected.

"Don't look so down," Santiago said. "Things are moving." He hugged her. Keeping his hands on her shoulders, he asked, "Now tell me exactly what part of the ranch Byron searched."

"The area we call Smokestack Rocks because the land formation looks sort of like chimneys. You know where that is?"

"Yes."

Santiago had uttered that single word with so much satisfaction that Jane knew it wasn't even close to the hiding place.

"Thank you, Jane." He gave her a resounding kiss and ran to the truck.

"Where are you going?"

"To keep an eye on the sheriff. Remember, you have a cell phone. Call me if anyone else comes."

"When will you be back? Lunch is ready," she called after him, but she doubted he heard her as he sped off, gravel spewing in all directions. What was it with men and trucks and speed? And with playing elaborate, dangerous versions of hide-and-seek?

Chapter Thirteen

Marisa was cranky. She also felt hot to the touch. When Jane took her temperature, it was 103 degrees, nearly causing Jane to drop the thermometer. She grabbed the phone and dialed her neighbor's number.

"Penny, I just took Marisa's temperature. It's one hundred and three. Isn't that awfully high?"

"For an adult that would be serious. For a baby it's not uncommon. Does she have any other symptoms?"

"Like what?"

"Throwing up? Diarrhea? A cough?"

"No." Jane made up her mind. "I'm taking her to the clinic."

"That's not a bad idea, but don't freak out. It's probably something she'll get over in a couple of days."

Jane phoned the clinic and was informed that there would be a wait but to come on in.

The wait turned out to be an hour long. Jane, not wanting to expose Marisa to a waiting room full of sick children and adults, gave the receptionist her cell number and waited outside. To pacify the baby, Jane paced up and down the sidewalk with her. Fortunately it was shaded by a couple of trees.

"Well, we meet again."

Jane, wondering if the male voice had spoken to her, turned around. It had. "Hello . . . Mr. Montgomery, was it?"

"Jack Montgomery," he said. He lit a cigarette. "What brings you to town?"

"We have an appointment with the pediatrician."

"Nothing serious, I hope."

"Routine." Jane wasn't quite sure why she was being evasive

140

with the man except that he raised all sorts of warning signals in her. Why that should be, she wasn't quite sure. He was neatly dressed in a western-style shirt and a string tie. He could easily pass for a Texas businessman. And yet he made her uneasy. His head made the turtle move, reminding her that Santiago knew him and didn't like him.

Casually she glanced around. Enough people entered and left the clinic and the adjoining pharmacy that she didn't think he was a danger to her. Why should he be? She didn't even know him. But Santiago did. She sensed they had a history—and it wasn't a friendly one.

He stood between her and the entrance to the clinic. Had he chosen that position deliberately? Why wasn't he going away? It wasn't as if they had anything to say to each other. She glanced at him again. Today she could see his eyes. They were the pale blue of a winter sky and held just about as much warmth.

"Excuse me," she said, trying to step around him.

"Just a minute."

He took a step closer and grabbed her arm. His fingers bit into her flesh. Jane repressed a groan of pain.

"I want you to give El Lobo a message. We want what belongs to us. If he tells us where it is, we'll leave, and no hard feelings."

What a liar. Judging by his expression, his body language, she doubted he was the forgiving-and-forgetting kind. He was so close that she was forced to inhale his scent, which reminded her of rancid cooking oil. Jane shuddered with distaste and tried to pull away. He pressed her arm harder.

"You know what to tell El Lobo?" he demanded. He blew cigarette smoke into her face.

"Yes." Jane twisted her body and moved the baby as far away from him and his cigarette as she could.

"If he doesn't cooperate, all sorts of unpleasant things will happen." He touched Marisa's head. "And not just to him."

"Don't touch the baby. Ever." Her voice came out low, mean, snarly.

"Ah, your vulnerable spot."

He said that with a grimace that was supposed to be a smile. Jane jerked her arm free, and, skirting around him, she rushed into the clinic.

Blast. She hadn't meant to reveal her love for Marisa quite so openly. It certainly made her vulnerable. She scolded herself until it occurred to her that this could hardly have been a secret. How many parents or surrogate parents didn't consider their children the most precious things on earth? Very few, and those few were undoubtedly aberrant.

What she should not have revealed was that he'd gotten to her. She loathed having given him that much power over her.

Inside, Jane had to wait some more. She didn't mind, as it gave her a chance to compose herself.

Jane liked the pediatrician. He told her that Marisa was suffering from roseola, a common and minor childhood disease. Her rash was just beginning to appear, which meant that she'd be back to normal in a couple of days.

The doctor's nurse set up a schedule of immunizations. Jane left the clinic much less worried than she had entered it. Except for Jack Montgomery and his nasty threats.

"She looks like she's feeling better," Santiago said, looking at the sleeping baby with loving eyes.

"Yes, she does. The doctor said she'd be her old self in a day or two."

They left the room, closing the door softly behind them.

Jane still had the dinner dishes to do, so she went back to the kitchen. Santiago followed her.

"You're upset," he said. "What's wrong, *querida?*"

She shrugged. "Why don't *you* tell me?"

"I would be happy to, if I knew what you wanted me to tell you."

Jane turned from the sink and faced him squarely. "I ran into Jack Montgomery, or whatever his name is, in town. I don't think the meeting was accidental, but how he knew I'd be going to the clinic I can't imagine. Anyway, he gave me a message for El Lobo. If you tell them where their stuff is, they'll go away quietly. What is it you have?"

Santiago shook his head in a disbelieving manner.

"I don't believe him about going away quietly and meekly either, but you have to give the stuff back," Jane said. "He threatened Marisa. Is he capable of hurting a baby?"

"There's no way he'll hurt Marisa. I won't let him."

"You didn't answer my question. Is he capable of hurting Marisa?" Santiago didn't say anything. His silence gave her the answer. Jane slumped into the nearest chair.

"I repeat: he isn't getting anywhere near Marisa. Why don't you believe that?"

Jane looked at him. At that moment he was like a stranger to her. "Because if he's determined enough, he can find a way. Nobody can protect anyone that well. You were in the 'danger business,' as you call it. If you wanted someone badly enough, couldn't you get him? Couldn't you?"

"Yes, but he isn't as good at the job as I am."

Santiago said this in a very matter-of-fact tone. He wasn't bragging, but that did not reassure her.

"You're gambling with her life. Is it worth it? Why not give them the pot and end it?" she demanded.

"Because that wouldn't end it. They would have to teach me a lesson, or try to, in order to keep others from doing what I did." Santiago sat beside her and took her hand. "Jane, we can't let them bring hundreds of pounds of drugs into the country. Think about it." When she didn't look convinced, he added, "In a few years Marisa will be in school. You want her to be able to buy the stuff on the playground?"

"No! Dear heaven above, no!" With her free hand, she rubbed her temple, trying to ease the pounding of the headache, trying to obliterate the images flitting through her head.

"I know I am asking a lot of you. But I need you to be strong and brave a little while longer. Can you do that? For Marisa? For me? For us?"

"I don't know. I'll try," she said.

"Thank you, *querida*." Santiago raised her hand and kissed it.

Jane found the courtly gesture not only sweet and endearing, but seductive. Quickly she got up and walked to the sink.

"I'll help you with the dishes," Santiago offered.

Jane had just finished applying hoof oil to the last horse when Father Anselmo's station wagon came to a stop in front of the corral. Jane picked up the grooming kit and joined the padre.

"I haven't seen you in church for a while," he said.

Jane blushed with guilt. "I know. We've been very busy."

"You've never been too busy to come to church on Sunday."

"I'll try to do better," she promised. She'd go to church on Sunday even though she couldn't bring herself to go to confession. Lying to Father Anselmo was monstrously wrong, and yet she couldn't tell him about her sham marriage. Was it pride? she wondered guiltily. Was she too proud to admit that a man like Santiago didn't find her attractive enough to insist she become his wife? He'd kissed her, and she hadn't exactly beaten him off with a stick. But he hadn't overridden any feeble protestations and excuses she'd come up with, hadn't picked her up and carried her off. That was her ultimate fantasy: Santiago sweeping her up in his arms like Rhett Butler had Scarlett and carrying her to his bed, obliterating the ugly reality of drug smugglers and danger.

"I brought you something," he said. "Or, rather, someone."

Intrigued, she watched him remove a pet carrier from the back of the station wagon.

"You didn't!" Jane exclaimed with a smile. "I was just telling Santiago that you threatened to bring me a whole litter of puppies."

"Just one dog. This is Kiley. Her owners moved away and couldn't take her. She's a good watchdog and good with kids. Come on, girl." The padre tugged gently on the leash to coax Kiley out of the carrier.

Though of uncertain pedigree, the dog's broad chest suggested that a Lab was among its forefathers. Jane held out her hand so Kiley could sniff it.

"She isn't very big or fierce looking," she said, her voice skeptical.

"That's the kind of dog you have to watch. What she lacks in size she makes up for in spirit and intelligence."

"I suppose I should keep her tied up for a couple of days till she realizes she lives here."

"Probably. I brought you a bag of dog food. She's used to being fed twice a day. Where do you want the food?"

"In the tack room. Come on, girl." Jane took the leash and tied it to a twenty-foot length of rope, which she then tied to one of the porch pillars. "This will give her some space to move. Father Anselmo, do you have time for coffee?"

"Not really." He looked around. "I take it Santiago is out on the range?"

"Yes, and Marisa is taking a nap." Jane patted the dog's silky head. "Thanks for Kiley."

"You're welcome. She needed a home, and you needed a dog." The padre studied Jane's face. Finally he said, "Why don't you just say what's sticking in your throat?"

"Do you know what Santiago is involved in?"

"More or less."

"Then you know it's dangerous. I've suggested he should let the authorities handle it, but he refuses. Says he doesn't know whom he can trust." Jane paused. "I'm not sure that's the real reason. Or the only reason."

Father Anselmo nodded. "I think you're right. Ask him. He's your husband. He owes you the truth."

Jane watched the padre drive away. If Santiago were really her husband, she could insist on knowing the truth. But he wasn't. He was . . . what? A familiar stranger with whom she shared a house? Of whom she grew fonder every day? *Fonder?* A euphemism, surely. The way her heart beat faster when she caught sight of him unexpectedly, the way she trembled when he touched her casually, the way he monopolized her thoughts—all these were symptoms of falling in love. Heaven help her.

With a sigh she sat on the bottom step of the porch, propped her elbows on her knees, and stared at the ground. A moment later Kiley came and stood in front of her as if waiting for permission to join Jane.

"Sit, girl," she invited. "Let me tell you about your new home. We have horses, cattle, and chickens. You've already met me. Then there's a darling little girl in the house who will adore you. And I hope you'll adore and protect her. Then there's Santiago. I don't know where to begin to tell you about him. Let's just say he's complicated. And wonderful. And sexy. And intelligent. And stubborn. And—well, you get the drift. I'll let you make up your mind about him."

Jane patted the dog's head before she went into the house.

Santiago was delighted with the dog and she with him. That didn't surprise Jane. Kiley was a female, wasn't she? Females of all ages, and apparently of all species, liked him.

Lying in bed that night, unable to sleep because of the heat and her worrisome thoughts, Jane reviewed her day. Or at least those parts that included Santiago. His refusal to ask for help from the authorities bothered her the most. True, he had fortified the house and its surroundings so that no sneak attack was possible.

The house had survived attacks by bandits and renegades from both sides of the border in the old days. Could she defend it single-handedly if necessary? Probably. At least for a while. The six-minute warning would allow her to close and lock the heavy, metal-enforced shutters that had withstood bullets in the past and should do so again.

By the time the two-minute warning went off, she would be in position by the front door with various weapons beside her. She knew she could hit the buried explosives in the yard with her first bullets. That should discourage the attackers and with luck disable a few of them. She could hold on till Santiago heard the shots and came rushing from the range.

Or she could contact the authorities and ask for help. As tempting as that was, she couldn't do it. Santiago would never forgive her. Whatever score he had to settle was extremely important to him. Important enough to risk everything.

Carefully, Jane lowered the sleeping baby into her crib. Marisa had been fussy all day, needing a little extra attention. Her rash was fading. According to the pediatrician, Marisa should be fine by morning.

Jane closed the door softly behind her. She was about to go to her bedroom when she heard an odd noise. Following it to the kitchen, she found Santiago sitting at the table, the old manual typewriter before him.

"I thought you had gone to bed, *querida.* Is my typing disturbing you?"

"No, not at all."

"But something is wrong. Tell me."

Jane shrugged. "It's silly. I mean, dreams aren't really omens, even if you have the same dream over and over."

"I take it that this recurring dream isn't pleasant. Tell me about this nightmare." Santiago made an inviting gesture toward the chair next to him.

Jane sat. "Are you a dream analyst in addition to being a cowboy, a fighter—"

"A lover, an uncle, a husband," he finished for her.

He was an uncle and technically a husband but not a lover. At least not hers.

"About your bad dream?" he prompted.

"You really want to hear about it?"

"Yes, or I wouldn't have asked."

"I dream I am in a strange city. It is night, and there are no stars and no moon. I am in a desperate hurry to get somewhere, but I am lost and I am scared. There is no one I can ask for directions." Jane shrugged. "That's a very common dream. Probably universal."

Santiago nodded. "Fear of being lost, either literally or metaphorically, is something we all have felt. Which do you fear more?"

"I have a good sense of direction," she said.

"Me too. It's the metaphorical loss of direction in our lives that we fear most."

"Father Anselmo probably thinks I'm well on my way to getting lost. He noticed I haven't been to church recently. I'd better go on Sunday, but he'll be disappointed again."

"Why?" Santiago asked, puzzled.

"Because I can't go to confession."

He noticed that this bothered her a great deal. He pulled his chair closer to hers. "Why can't you? I cannot imagine you having done something so heinous that you can't confess it to your priest."

"How about this lie we're living?"

Santiago concentrated all his attention, all his senses on Jane. What was she trying to tell him? Gently, his fingers stroked her bare arm.

"If I went to confession, I'd have to admit that I lied to the INS, to Mrs. Winter, to everyone."

"Not necessarily."

Her face blanched. "I can't lie in the confessional," she whispered, shocked.

She looked at him with stricken eyes that cut him to the quick. Hastily he added, "No, that's not what I meant to suggest." He kissed the soft skin on her wrist and felt her tremble.

"What did you mean?"

"That things don't have to stay as they are. Actually, nothing remains the same. Change is a law of nature. Change, adapt, or die," Santiago said.

"Isn't that a rather grim way of looking at life?"

"Not necessarily. Change comes naturally. Take us," he said, and he lifted her chin so he could look into her eyes. "A few months ago you lived alone in this house. Now you share it with a baby and a man. Is that scary? No, don't answer that," he said quickly. "Bad example because of the smugglers. But imagine us here without the smuggling. Would that be scary?"

"Just a little," she admitted.

"I know you love Marisa. You can't possibly find her scary,

so it must be me." While he waited for her to speak, he took her hand and laid it against his cheek. "Why am I scary?" He moved the palm of her hand to his mouth and pressed a kiss against her warm skin.

"Because you're a man."

Santiago studied her face intently. "You don't strike me as a woman who fears men."

"I don't exactly. Only what might happen. I have one unhappy marriage behind me—"

"So have I. You think because of that we're automatically doomed to another unhappy marriage?"

Jane shrugged.

"Are you the same woman you were in that marriage?"

"No. Oh, no!"

"Exactly. We have maturity, experience, tolerance, patience, and understanding on our side. With all those qualities, think what we can do. What you and I can become for each other."

His eyes focused on her mouth. Jane could almost feel his lips against hers. She was quickly moving beyond the ability to think clearly. Way beyond. There wasn't a cell in her body that wasn't aware of him. Every nerve ending hummed and vibrated in anticipation and need. His tawny eyes had darkened. Looking into their depths robbed her of the ability to speak.

"Jane, take a chance on us," he said, his voice low, coaxing. "Things will change between us eventually."

Eventually. How far in the future was *eventually?* What a wishy-washy sort of word. She felt like weeping but determinedly repressed the tears. She nodded. Whispering, "Good night," she retreated to her room.

Take a chance on us. Part of her would like nothing better than to take a chance, but another part of her was afraid. She had failed once. Could she risk failing again?

She knew Santiago was waiting for her answer. How long would he wait?

Chapter Fourteen

No matter how hard she tried, Jane could no longer ignore the tempting aroma of strong, freshly brewed coffee. Reluctantly, she got out of bed and put on her robe. The first thing she saw in the kitchen was Santiago, holding a mug of coffee. He seemed deep in thought.

When he saw her, he smiled. "You're up. I made coffee, good and strong, the way you like it." He filled a mug and handed it to her.

"Thank you." She blew on the coffee to help it cool down.

"What time is it?"

"Around six."

"What? By six the horses are fed already and—"

"Not today," Santiago said.

"Why didn't you wake me?"

"Because you needed the rest."

"That's no reason to make the horses suffer, just because you thought I was tired."

"The horses are sleek and well fed. Waiting an extra hour is not going to harm them. Or even waiting two hours—"

"It's not going to take me that long to drink the coffee."

Halfway through the morning the six-minute warning alarm went off, sending Jane into her well-practiced defense mode. When she recognized her neighbor's truck, she quickly took off the gun belt. By the time Penny knocked on the door, Jane had stowed her arsenal in the hall closet.

"Hey, Jane. I came by to see how the baby's doing."

"She seems fine this morning. Come and see." Jane led the

way into the kitchen, where Marisa was banging a spoon against the side of the playpen.

"Well, hi there, you little sweetie," Penny cooed. "Can I pick her up?"

"I'd rather you didn't. I spoiled her a little while she was sick, and now she expects to get held all the time. I'm trying to get back into our routine."

"I understand. Believe me, I do. I had three babies in six years. I thought I'd never get anything done but tending the little ones. I love my girls, but I'm glad they're growing up."

Jane filled two mugs with coffee and handed one to Penny. Then she continued to peel the potatoes she had boiled earlier.

"What're you making?" Penny asked.

"Potato salad for supper. To go with some leftover ham." Jane sighed. "It's hard to come up with ideas for meals every day. I don't mind cooking if someone just told me what to fix."

"Tell me about it," Penny said in heartfelt agreement. "When I ask Tom what he wants, he says, 'I dunno. Whatever.' So he gets a lot of 'whatever.'"

The women smiled at each other.

"I remember when you were single. You'd cook one meal a day," Penny said. "The rest of the time you'd fix a salad or a sandwich or a bowl of cereal." Penny looked at Jane shrewdly. "Your new husband doesn't go for that?"

"I don't know. I haven't asked him. I figure he works hard, so he deserves a good meal."

"He's out on the range? Whereabout?" Penny asked.

"I'm not exactly sure. He's mending fences, so he could be anywhere. You know how fences are forever in need of repair."

"Yeah, I know. He didn't give you some idea where he'd be in case of an emergency?"

Jane thought for a moment. "He may have mentioned the south range." She didn't add that she hadn't paid much attention, being too busy wondering when if ever she could kiss him good-bye before he left.

Penny looked around the kitchen. "Did you see the flyer

with the ads from the appliance store in town? They're having a big sale. Now that you have a husband, why don't you get him to buy you a new stove and fridge? One you don't have to defrost? It would make lots less work for you."

"Having a husband doesn't automatically mean that we have more money," Jane said.

"Men can always find ways to get some extra income if they're motivated enough. And it's up to us women to motivate them," Penny said with a wink. "Well, I'd better go."

Jane watched her drive off. Ordinarily Penny wasn't a curious neighbor, but this morning she'd been full of questions. How odd. Jane shook her head and dismissed Penny's curiosity.

An hour or so later, she put the baby into her stroller and pushed her across the yard toward the tack room.

A flash of light from the direction of the county road caught her attention. A flash like sunlight hitting glass, a mirror, or shiny metal. Jane listened intently, but she didn't hear the sound of a car or truck engine. There was nothing else in that direction that should have caused that flash. Maybe she had imagined it. Just as she was trying to convince herself of that, she saw the flash again.

Someone was spying on her through binoculars. The person was either careless or didn't mind if she knew she was being watched. Her scalp tightened in alarm.

Quickly, without seeming to hurry, she grabbed as many bridles as she could carry in one arm and still push the stroller with the other. Crossing the yard, she forced herself not to look in the direction of the flash, nor to hurry. She carried Marisa and the bridles inside.

Though the shutters were partially closed against the day's heat, she closed them completely and locked them in all the rooms except the one window in the kitchen that faced the yard. Her defense window.

To put the baby out of the line of fire from the window, Jane dragged the playpen into a corner of the kitchen. She set Paco's cage next to the baby. Then Jane called Santiago on the cell phone, but he was obviously out of range. She was on her own. *The attic.* From there she'd have a good view of the land.

In the hall closet she pulled down the narrow ladder. With Santiago's binoculars around her neck and carrying the shotgun in her free hand, she climbed into the attic.

She made her way to the small window in the back gable that faced southeast, the direction of the flashes. Methodically she swept the binoculars over the land, starting at the horizon and working her way toward the house. Moments later, she saw the blue sedan. It took a little longer to locate the man, as his khaki pants and pale green shirt blended into the landscape.

From the angle of the attic window, he appeared in the extreme left edge of her field of vision. Slowly, she panned the area with the binoculars, but there was no one else. At least no one she could see. Jane concentrated on the man. With the binoculars raised to his eyes, his beige hat pulled low, and the distance between them, he could be anybody. Frustrated, she muttered some uncomplimentary things about him.

Why was he watching the house? Was he planning to drive up and attack if he didn't see Santiago? Or attack if he did see Santiago?

She heard the phone ring. Since she couldn't get down in time, she let the machine pick up the message.

The decision to leave the attic was made for her when Marisa started to fuss in earnest. Jane climbed down the stairs, set the shotgun next to the front door, took the .38 from the cookie tin, and placed it next to the Colt and gun belt on the counter. Only then did she pick up the baby to comfort her.

Sitting at the kitchen table, she gave Marisa a bottle of apple juice. Then she listened to the phone message. Father Anselmo wanted Santiago to give him a call around six.

"What shall we do, baby girl? Santiago won't be back for hours. We are being spied on by some man, and I don't think he's watching us because he likes us. We could make a run for it in the truck. No. He's too close to the road leading to the highway. He could catch us.

"If I were by myself, I'd try luring him to follow me cross-country. He'd break an axle or tear up the undercarriage of his car in no time. I mean, who drives a fancy sedan off the road in rough country like ours? Only a city guy who doesn't know any better."

Jane considered her options. She couldn't reach Santiago. She could phone the sheriff's office. Talk to Bud Wilson. But what would she say? There's a guy on her land watching her house through binoculars? Technically that might be a misdemeanor, but was it enough to send a deputy from an under-staffed office all the way to her ranch? Doubtful.

"I guess we'll stay put. The house has thick stone walls and strong shutters, and I'm a good shot. My great-great-great grandmother—maybe it's only two greats." Jane shrugged. "Anyway, she held off a couple of horse thieves from this very kitchen window. I figure I can do the same. But just in case, I'll try reaching Santiago again." He was still out of range.

Jane changed the baby's diaper before she put Marisa back into the playpen. Then she climbed up into the attic again.

The man was gone. Jane examined the land slowly and thoroughly, but all she saw was a faint plume of dust. The intruder driving away? *If only,* she prayed. She ran downstairs, unlocked the door, and cautiously stepped onto the porch, shotgun at the ready.

She saw nothing out of the ordinary. Besides, the alarm system hadn't gone off. Temporarily relieved, she went back into the house.

Tonight Santiago would be with them. Amazing how the mere thought of him made her feel safe and cherished. She jumped a foot when the phone rang.

"Jeez. Get a grip," she muttered. She picked up the receiver. "Hello?" Silence. "Hello? Is anyone there?" Jane thought she heard breathing but wasn't sure. Quickly she hung up. Someone trying to rattle her? The man with the binoculars?

"Nice try," she muttered.

"May as well work on the bridles," Jane said. Doing something normal like working on leather was exactly what she needed to calm herself. But even that familiar task didn't lift the sense of unease that had settled in her stomach like a big rock.

The phone rang again. This time she let the machine pick it up.

"Jane, are you there? Pick up."

Penny. She grabbed the receiver. "I'm here."

"Good. Santiago just called here. He must have been out of range of your place. He's had some trouble—"

"What kind of trouble?" Jane asked, her throat constricted by fear.

"I'm not sure. He kept fading in and out. You know how these cell phones are. He said to bring the horse and meet him at the base of Three-Cornered Hat Ridge."

"What was he doing way over there?"

"I don't know. As I said, he kept fading out. I think he said something happened to his horse. Shall I send Christie over to bring Marisa to our place?"

"Can't Christie babysit her over here?"

"She's got a ton of homework. If the baby's at our place, I can help watch her."

"All right. Please send Christie right away. I'll get Marisa ready. And thanks, Penny."

Jane flew into action. She packed the diaper bag with essentials and two jars of baby food. Then she changed clothes.

Impatiently Jane waited on the porch for Christie. She petted Kiley and told the dog to watch the house.

Marisa fussed a little when she handed her to the babysitter, but the prospect of a ride in the truck soon distracted her.

Jane hitched the trailer to the truck, grabbed the first-aid kit for horses, two canteens of water, and the shotgun. Then she sped off toward the mountains.

Once she left the main road, she had to slow down to fifteen miles an hour because the trail was little more than old tire tracks on the rocky terrain. She fumed with impatience and worry.

What had happened? Had Santiago's horse stepped into a

chuck hole? Been spooked by a rattler? Had the truck broken down? Penny hadn't really been sure what Santiago had said due to the poor reception. Jane stopped the truck and tried the cell phone again. No luck. Shouldn't he be in range by now? The closer she got to her destination, the more anxious she became.

When the trail ended at the foot of the rock formation, Jane parked the truck and got out. She looked around. Santiago could be behind any of the big boulders. Cupping her hands around her mouth, she called his name. When she heard a faint reply, she sprinted in the direction of the sound.

Every time she thought she came nearer to the voice answering her, she had to climb yet higher. Rather out of breath, she rounded another boulder. Something snaked out, grabbed her, and slammed her face-first against the boulder. She cried out in pain and fear. Her arms were twisted behind her back.

"Be still," a man's voice growled.

"Who are you? What do you want? And where's Santiago?" Jane asked, her voice shaky.

"I don't know where Santiago is. Yet. And we want you."

The man spun her around. He took two steps back.

"You!" Jane was about to fling herself at him and demand an explanation when Jack Montgomery raised the pistol and aimed it at her face.

Looking into the barrel of the gun, she swallowed hard. Foolishly she had left her gun in the truck, but the way he had grabbed her, she wouldn't have been able to use it anyway.

"I didn't think it would be this easy to get you," he said with grin.

He looked like a grinning turtle. Jane hated his grin. Nothing would have given her greater pleasure than to wipe it off his face. *Not yet.* "That wasn't Santiago phoning my neighbor, was it?"

"Nope. With a cell phone it isn't hard to fool someone."

"Was it your man, spying on our house?"

He frowned. "How do you know about that?"

"Carelessness. Sunlight flashing on glass."

He swore. "Stupid. Stupid."

"Good help is hard to find."

Montgomery glowered at her.

"What do you want with me?" she demanded, her voice stronger and steadier now.

"All in good time. Back up against the boulder, and turn around."

Jane didn't move. She cast a quick glance around her, weighing her options. The truck was too far away and the man with the gun too close for her to make a break for it.

"Move. Now," he ordered.

Patience wasn't his strong point. Something to remember and maybe use against him. With the gun pointing at her unwaveringly, she had no choice but to obey.

"Don't even think of bolting," he warned. "I'll shoot you in the leg before you get six feet and then make you walk on that leg all over this mountain. I guarantee that won't be any fun."

From his voice, Jane knew he would do exactly that. But he wouldn't kill her. At least not yet. Whatever Montgomery's plan was, he needed her alive.

"Ouch!" Jane yelled, pretending he was tying her wrists too tightly. She thought he loosened the rope just a bit. Enough to give her wiggle room and work her hands free?

"Turn around, and start walking."

"Where to?"

He gestured with the gun. "That way."

They weren't going up the mountain but walking parallel to its crest. Where were they going? There was nothing in these mountains. There was no trail, just uneven, rocky terrain. Jane stumbled several times.

"Can't you walk any faster?" he demanded.

"No. You try walking with your hands tied behind you. It upsets your balance. If you must tie my hands, at least tie them in front. That way I might walk faster." Miraculously, he seemed to be considering that. Jane held her breath.

"Okay. Stop." Montgomery stepped behind her and put the pistol into the pocket of his Windbreaker. He untied her hands. "Don't try anything," he warned her again, coming around to her front. "Hold out your hands."

Jane did. Unfortunately, that didn't bring him close enough for her to administer a good, strong kick to his crotch.

"Where are we going?" she asked again.

"To my camp."

"Why?"

"Because it'll be dark soon. I don't aim to stumble around this mountain at night. Too easy to lose you."

"You intend to keep me at your camp?"

"Yes."

"What for?"

"Bait. Or trade goods."

"Bait?"

"For Santiago. I figure your husband will come after you. Or, if he's smart, he'll trade. Give us back what belongs to us in exchange for you."

"What makes you think he'll do either?"

"He might not trade, but he'll come for you. He's got a sense of honor that'll demand he come. He can't help himself."

Montgomery was probably right. Jane shivered. Santiago might walk right into a trap. She couldn't lose him. Sometime during the long night ahead she would have to find a way to escape. Or disable Montgomery.

As soon as Santiago parked the truck in the yard, he had a bad feeling. Something was not right. Jane's truck was gone, as was the other horse trailer. She might have driven the truck somewhere, but she had no reason to take the trailer. What had happened?

He rushed into the kitchen. There was no note on the table where Jane usually left notes. He noticed the flashing light on the answering machine. After listening to Father Anselmo's message, he dialed the padre's number. As soon as they had exchanged greetings, Santiago asked, "Father, have you heard from Jane today?"

"No. I phoned and left a message earlier. Why? What's wrong?"

"She's gone."

"What do you mean gone?"

"As in not being at the ranch. Her truck is gone. She didn't leave a note. She always does."

"Marisa? Did she take the baby with her?"

"Yes."

"Then she probably went to the neighbors' place. Or into town," Father Anselmo said.

"The other horse trailer is gone too. That makes no sense, and that's what worries me."

"Phone the Longs. And then call me back and let me know what you found out," Father Anselmo said.

Santiago dialed the neighbors' number. One of the girls answered.

"Is Jane there?"

"No. But Mom might know something. I'll get her."

Santiago waited, drumming his fingers impatiently on the kitchen counter. Hadn't he warned Jane not to leave the safety of the ranch? She was a smart woman. She understood the danger, the need for caution. Then what had happened to make her leave? *If something happened to her, if . . .* Ruthlessly he stopped those thoughts. *Think positive. Nothing can happen to Jane. She's too dear, too precious, too—*

"Santiago? What can I do for you?" Penny asked.

"Jane isn't at the ranch. Do you know where she and Marisa went?"

"Marisa is here with us, and Jane drove out to help you after you phoned our place. What's wrong?"

Santiago felt the blood drain from his heart. He knew he swayed. He gripped the edge of the counter and closed his eyes. Somehow they had succeeded in luring Jane away from the house. He took a breath before he spoke.

"Penny, tell me exactly what happened."

She reported in detail, concluding, "So then she rode out to Three-Cornered Hat Ridge to help you."

"About what time was that?" When Penny told him, he drew his first hopeful breath. Only a couple of hours. They could not travel too far from Three-Cornered Hat Ridge. Not in the dark. That would narrow his search. Making a fast decision, he said, "Father Anselmo will come to get Marisa."

"We can keep her," Penny said.

"I know, and thank you, but Father Anselmo is looking forward to spending time with her." Santiago hung up. For a moment he stared at the phone in his hand. Then he phoned the padre and told him what had happened.

After a moment of shocked silence, Father Anselmo asked, "What can I do?"

"Get Marisa and keep her with you. Please do not let her go with anyone, no matter how much they assure you that either Jane or I want her. Can you do that for me?"

"Of course. I'll drive out to the Longs' the moment I hang up the phone. You think Jane was taken as a hostage?"

"Probably."

"What are you going to do?"

"Find her."

"You know they're setting a trap for you," the padre said.

"Yes, and they'll pay dearly for taking Jane."

"Santiago, revenge is a double-edged sword. It takes as big a toll on he who exacts it as on him on whom it is visited."

"Father, it's not revenge but justice. Listen, I have things to prepare. Thanks for your help with Marisa."

"No problem. I'll say a few prayers for you and Jane."

Chapter Fifteen

Jane tried to get comfortable on the blanket Montgomery had tossed at her an hour earlier. After a while she gave up and pretended to be asleep. The physical discomfort would keep her from actually falling asleep, which was exactly what she wanted.

Montgomery sat on his sleeping bag, smoking a cigarette. Earlier she had overheard him speaking on his cell phone, so she knew he was waiting for a call from someone who appeared to be his boss. When his phone chirped, she lay very still, forcing herself to breathe in that regular, shallow fashion that mimicked sleep.

"Hold on a second," Montgomery said.

He approached Jane. Bending down, he listened for a moment. Then he walked a few feet away. "She's out like a light. I made her walk a long way."

He listened for a moment while Jane strained to hear his side of the conversation.

"You think it's working? He'll come after her?"

Silence again. Jane virtually held her breath.

"Expect him by morning? You don't think he'll come during the night?"

Silence again.

"Yeah. I guess you're right. Not even El Lobo can track in the dark."

Another minute of silence.

"I understand. I'll take care of him. And then of her. No witnesses."

Jane's breath caught. She hoped it hadn't been an audible

gasp. When Montgomery didn't react, she breathed again. She heard what sounded like a snort.

"Of course I can do this. It's hardly my first hit. It's not like I'm a virgin. And no matter what you think, El Lobo is not Superman. I'll get him."

A cold shiver shook Jane. If Montgomery had his way, neither she nor Santiago would live beyond tomorrow morning.

Montgomery approached her. She felt him standing over her for a moment. Then he walked away. She heard him settle himself into his sleeping bag. Shortly thereafter, the sound of snoring assured her that it was time to go into action.

She turned until she was almost flat on her stomach, trying to locate the sharpest of the objects under her blanket that pocked her painfully. She paused every few seconds to be sure Montgomery was still snoring. She discarded several rocks before she found a flat metal disk. The top of a can, judging by the sharp edge. Perfect, if she didn't slice off a finger first.

It took a half dozen tries before she had positioned herself so that she could rub the metal against the rope binding her hands. She checked her progress from time to time. Dismayed, she realized it would take her the greater part of the night to saw through the rope. Still, it was better to do something to free herself than to wait idly for Montgomery to kill Santiago and then her.

The thought of leaving Marisa without a family refueled her energy and determination. From time to time she had to stop because her fingers became numb with fatigue. She tracked the movement of the moon across the night sky. Just as she despaired of making sufficient progress before dawn, she felt the first strands of the rope fray and then break.

Renewed energy surged through her. She was going to make it. She would escape and keep Santiago from running into an ambush.

Grim-faced, with single-minded determination, Santiago prepared for battle as he had done innumerable times during the past half decade of his life. Only this time the stakes were higher. So much higher. He was fighting for Jane—the woman he wanted, needed. The woman without whom he could no longer envision life.

Dressed in camouflage fatigues, he carefully stowed the battle gear in the various pockets of his outfit. He blackened his face, then strapped on the sidearm, knife, and canteen. He picked up the M-16 and stepped outside.

Under the starry sky, he breathed easier. In the house the lingering presence of Jane had dogged his every step. With each breath he took, he'd filled his body, his mind, his soul with the very essence of her. That was both excruciatingly painful and exquisitely pleasurable.

Briefly he closed his eyes, willing himself to slip into his warrior role where all emotion ceased, where Jane became the objective to be attained and the abductor the opposition to be vanquished. In his mind he reduced the mission to the unemotional steps of goal, opposition, victory.

Because sound carried far in the night, he knew he would have to abandon the truck a good distance from Three-Cornered Hat Ridge. The rest of the way he would go on horseback and then on foot. He saddled Jane's fastest horse and led her into the trailer.

"We're going to find Jane, so don't let me down, girl." The mare nickered softly as if she understood. He loaded his gear, food, and water. Earlier he had forced himself to eat some of the ham and potato salad Jane had made. He hadn't been hungry, but knew he would need every ounce of energy and strength. And because Jane had made it, the food not only provided nutritional value but assumed symbolic sustenance.

He waited until the full moon was high in the sky before he left the ranch, driving with the headlights turned off. All the time he had spent familiarizing himself with the trails on the ranch would pay off now.

Jane was a brave woman, but she had only expected to find him and a lame horse or a busted truck, not a man or men lurking behind rocks with weapons drawn and ready to use.

Santiago smacked his fist repeatedly against the steering

wheel. Then, taking a deep breath, he vowed that that was the last outburst he would allow himself. No more emotions. Only cold reason and steel-edged resolve.

Leaving the truck, Santiago proceeded on horseback. Riding would take longer, but it was safer if he hoped to have the element of surprise on his side. Half an hour later, he found Jane's truck and trailer. He let the mare out. She'd find her way home. Jane had left the key in the truck as well as her cell phone, indicating haste and concern. For him. He felt an unaccustomed tightness in his throat. He fought it down ruthlessly. *No time for feelings,* he reminded himself again—not until Jane was safe at home and his enemies were dead.

The moon was near the end of her night's journey. A couple of hours more and the sun would rise, Jane estimated, and she redoubled her efforts. With a sudden snap, the last fibers of the rope broke. She felt like shouting. Instead, she whispered a fast prayer. She rubbed her wrists. Then she drew her knees to her chest and fumbled with the rope that bound her feet. She didn't dare sit up until she was ready to run for her life. Moments later, she had untied the rope.

Jane flexed her ankles to restore circulation. While she did this, she considered her next step: steal away silently, quickly, or hit Montgomery over the head with a rock to keep him from following her? But even as she toyed with the thought of hitting him, she knew she couldn't do it. Not in cold blood. Heaven knew Montgomery wasn't destined for sainthood, but his life wasn't hers to take.

That left creeping away. Whisper-quiet, she moved the blanket a few feet, where she draped it over some rocks. In the dark and from a distance, it looked as if it covered a sleeping body. If Montgomery woke before daylight, that should fool him.

On her hands and knees she crawled, clearing the way in front of her so she wouldn't dislodge a rock and wake him. Unfortunately he had bedded down between her and the way to the truck. The rough trail was narrow. She would have to pass within striking distance of him. She didn't dare risk that. She had no choice but to go south. Once she was far enough away, she could go east a bit and double back to the truck.

Jane glanced back. Estimating that the distance she'd crawled would have safely brought her out of his hearing range, she got to her feet and walked as fast as the rough terrain and the thin moonlight permitted.

Where was Santiago? Had he figured out that she had walked into a trap? Part of her hoped he hadn't, that he was safe at the ranch. Even as she wished for that, she knew she was hoping for the impossible. Santiago was probably already on his way to Three-Cornered Hat Ridge or would be by the first light of day. That he would come after her she didn't doubt for a minute.

The next path leading down the ridge was at Silver Spring, which was probably four or five miles farther south. It would take her a good hour to reach it. Too long. She had to get off the ridge now. Looking at the steep downward incline, she took a couple of deep breaths before she started.

Halfway down, she lost her footing, fell backward, and slid down the ridge on her bottom until a good-sized rock stopped her fall. She lay stunned for a minute. Gingerly she rose and took inventory. Her hands were scratched and bleeding, and she hurt all over as if she had taken a horrific beating, but, miraculously, she hadn't broken any bones.

Now she had to make a crucial decision. She could go north to the truck, or she could head east for the ranch. The first choice would bring her dangerously close to Montgomery, and the second would expose her to a harsh environment without water. Could she make it back to the ranch? She hadn't slept, she hadn't eaten, and she hadn't drunk any water since last night.

Praying she wasn't making the wrong choice, she turned north toward her truck.

Santiago sat on the ground, his back resting against a rock. He had slapped the mare on her rump to send her back to the ranch. Now he waited. For the umpteenth time he glanced at the eastern horizon. Finally the first, gray-white light crept up and pushed back the darkness.

He rose and stretched. Then he walked to the path leading up the ridge. Just as he had guessed, he found a set of footprints. From the size he knew they belonged to Jane. Something about the small footprints tugged at his heart. She had hurried up the path and straight into danger because of him.

He followed her trail. Behind a boulder he found what he had expected but had been afraid to find: the scene of Jane's ambush. One man had grabbed her. That meant that they had sent one of their best. It didn't matter. To rescue her, Santiago was prepared to take on the devil himself.

Fifty yards up the trail he realized he had lost their tracks. Cursing, he hurried back to the boulder. Now that it was lighter, he saw the tracks veering off to the south. She had been forced to walk over rough terrain. He saw signs that she had stumbled.

Stay calm. Stay objective. Santiago murmured those words as if they were his mantra. He slowed his pace, exchanging speed for stealth and silence. They couldn't have walked much farther before darkness made it too dangerous to go on. Only a mountain goat could maneuver this terrain in the dark.

When he rounded a rock formation ten minutes later, he quickly jumped back. He had almost walked right into their camp. Cautiously he edged forward to take another look. He saw a sleeping bag and a small backpack beside it. Obviously the abductor's. Some twelve feet or so away, he saw a blanket spread over the rocky ground. The louse had made her lie on rocks. One more thing to add to the growing list of his sins.

There was no sign of Jane or her captor. Was this the trap he was supposed to walk into? If he were setting a trap, where would he position himself? *On high ground.* Santiago studied the terrain above the camp. Several boulders offered perfect cover for an ambusher.

Quietly, carefully, he climbed up the ridge until he was a good distance above the camp. Using his binoculars, he studied the terrain between him and the camp. He moved several times to look at the area from different angles. *Nobody.* Puzzled, he wondered where the man was.

And where was Jane? For the first time, gut-wrenching fear surged through him. What if the guy figured she had served her purpose and . . . *No.* He could not think like that. Jane was alive, and he would rescue her. He had to. He could not lose even one more person he cared about.

He hurried down the ridge to look at the camp for clues. The backpack contained bottles of water, granola bars, and bags of trail mix. The guy had left without his food and water, which made no sense unless he planned to return.

Because Santiago was worried and upset, he almost missed the tracks. Someone had gone down the steep hill from the camp. Going down without a rope and climbing equipment wasn't the smartest thing to do. Nor had he chosen the best spot for the descent. Both of these facts suggested that he had been in a great hurry. Why? What was the reason to take such chances? Whatever his reasons had been, Santiago's were equally desperate. Mentally plotting his route, he started down.

Jane watched her truck for several minutes from a safe distance even though she was thirsty and her mouth was so dry, she couldn't even wet her lips. Her canteen was in the truck. She forced herself to count to fifty before she approached the pickup. The first thing she did was take the .38 from its hiding place under the seat and slide it into her coat pocket. Then she grabbed the canteen and drank thirstily.

"Nothing has ever tasted this good," she murmured, capping the canteen.

"Isn't that the truth?"

Gasping, Jane whirled around and looked once more into the barrel of Montgomery's gun. "You," she said, defeat slamming through her. "How did you get here so fast?"

"Something woke me. I decided to check on you. Imagine my surprise when I didn't find you."

Rattler-fast, he slapped her across the face. The force of the blow threw Jane against the truck. The whole side of her face exploded with pain. It also roused her from that temporary feeling of defeat. Just then she could have torn him to pieces without a qualm.

"You ever pull a stunt like that again, I'll shoot you right then and there. You hear me?" Montgomery demanded.

Jane said nothing. If contempt could kill, Montgomery would have been incinerated on the spot. She felt blood trickle from her mouth. She pulled a tissue from her pocket and pressed it against her lips. *The gun. In her pocket.* She estimated that it would take her a couple of seconds to get it out and snap the safety off. Too long. Montgomery needed less than a second to pull the trigger.

He tied her hands in front. "Move," he ordered, pointing toward the ridge with his gun.

"Not again," Jane muttered.

"Get going. I'm not telling you a second time."

"You think Santiago is going to walk into your trap just like that? He isn't stupid, you know. Not even staking me out as your Judas goat will make him careless. He may not even come."

"He'll come."

"Because of me?"

Montgomery nodded. "And his machismo."

Jane flicked him a disbelieving look.

"What? You don't believe me? You will when he comes rushing to your rescue. Now move."

Jane picked up the canteen she had dropped when he had slapped her and started up the ridge once more. At least Montgomery had let her keep the water. He probably figured she wasn't going to live long enough for it to matter whether she had water or not.

"You know Santiago, don't you? From where?" she asked.

"We used to work together."

Jane stopped and stared at him.

"You don't believe me? Once upon a time I worked for the government too."

"What happened?" she asked.

"I discovered that the other side paid much better."

"You sold out for money?"

"Don't look so shocked. Money is the best, if not the only, thing worth selling out for. When you come right down to it, everybody can be bought. Everybody can be persuaded to sell out."

"You're quite the cynic, aren't you?"

"Wrong. I'm a realist. And in this world, the realists win."

Not if she could help it. She would have to find a way to warn Santiago. And stay alive at the same time. That wasn't going to be easy.

"Let's go," Montgomery ordered, and he motioned with his gun again.

While walking as slowly as she dared, Jane frantically considered various options. She could trip, fall, and claim she'd hurt her ankle and couldn't go on. No, he might just shoot her as if she were a horse.

"Can't you move any faster?" he demanded irritably.

"No."

"No? What do you mean, no?"

Jane stopped walking and looked at Montgomery defiantly.

"I mean I'm exhausted. I've walked all over this ridge, I haven't slept, and I haven't eaten. I'm beat." Jane sat down in the middle of the path.

"I don't believe this! I'm beginning to feel sorry for El Lobo, being stuck with such a mule-headed woman." Montgomery removed his hat and wiped his forehead with a sleeve of his shirt. Then slowly, as if talking to a child, he said, "See this gun? I'm pointing it at you. It's loaded. All I have to do is pull the trigger, and you're history. You get that?"

"But you need me alive to persuade Santiago to do something, right?"

Montgomery glowered at her. "Believe me, lady, that's the only reason you're still breathing."

"What is it you want Santiago to do?"

"Trade. Exchange. He's got something that belongs to us, and we want it back."

"So you think Santiago will make a trade? Me for your . . . What exactly is it he has?"

"Something worth a great deal of money."

Drugs, Jane guessed. Santiago must have taken the drugs from the camping party and hidden them somewhere on the range. That explained why suddenly several people had showed such a keen interest in her land: Byron, who claimed to have left something on the mesa, and the sheriff, who hadn't even bothered to explain his visit.

"And you think he's going to trade that valuable stuff for me?" Jane asked, her voice skeptical. "Get real. Would you?"

"No, but then, I'm not the Boy Scout he is," Montgomery said with a sneer.

Unlike Montgomery, Jane admired the ideals and values of the Boy Scouts. And, yes, Santiago had principles. And she loved him for them. Startled, she discovered that she had consciously admitted to herself that she loved him. She couldn't lose him. She had to do something to help him. *What?*

Then it hit her: do exactly what she had been doing. Slow down their progress up the ridge and prevent Montgomery from setting an elaborate, effective trap. Down here the terrain was more open and less suitable for an ambush.

"You said Santiago had something that belonged to *us*. So there are more people involved?"

"Yes."

"And they sent you . . . because?"

"Because I know him and because I'm good at what I do."

A good killer. Jane felt goose bumps pucker the skin on her arms. "You're not the big boss of the operation, are you?"

"I'm second in command."

"Does the big boss know Santiago?"

"Yes, but what difference does it make? For crissake. You're the nosiest woman I've met. Now shut up and move!"

Since his voice had turned snarly and mean, Jane rose and started to walk. She winced when he prodded her hard with the barrel of his gun. Another bruise to add to the ones she'd sustained when she'd slid down the ridge. She walked quietly for several minutes.

"Did the big boss work for the government too?"

"Yes."

"So you're both rogue agents."

"If you ask me one more question, I'm going to gag you."

He meant it. Jane shut her mouth but walked as slowly as she dared. Since she was tired, it wasn't difficult to pretend to be exhausted.

She ought to mark the trail so Santiago could find them more easily, but how? With her hands tied, all she could do was finger the front of her jacket. One of the buttons was loose. If she could rip it off and drop it, he might find it.

Through binoculars Santiago watched the man he had known as Tortuga, the man Jane knew as Jack Montgomery. When Jane turned her face a little, Santiago cursed volubly. One cheek was swollen, one eye was almost completely shut, and the sweet mouth Santiago loved to kiss was bloodied.

Before he knew what he was doing, he had the M-16 aimed at Montgomery. Although he was certain he could hit the man, he didn't dare shoot him. Not when he had a gun pointed at Jane's back. Not when there was even the slightest chance that Montgomery might pull the trigger reflexively as he went down.

There would be other, better chances. For now he had to be content to follow them, but before the day was over, Jane's tormentor would be dead. Or wish he were.

They walked on the trail that grew steeper and steeper. Jane no longer had to pretend she was exhausted. Each step was more difficult than the last.

"How much farther are we going? We're close to the top of the ridge. I'm not pretending when I say I'm going to collapse. You think Santiago will exchange your valuable stuff for a dead wife? Think again."

Montgomery looked around. "Okay. We'll go back to the camp. There's food there. And it's a good spot."

Jane swallowed hard. She didn't have to ask him what it was a good spot for—ambush and murder.

He motioned for her to walk, his gun trained on her. They continued until Jane was sure they had gone too far.

"I believe that last night we turned south before this."

"No. Turn by that rock ahead."

Jane knew this country better than Montgomery did. He was wrong. Still, arguing with an armed, crabby, and directionally challenged man wasn't the best idea.

They turned south. By the way Montgomery looked around, Jane suspected he realized they'd climbed too far. She kept glancing down the ridge, hoping to spot their camp. Suddenly she caught a flash of blue color on the ground. There was nothing blue in these mountains this time of year. At least nothing that belonged there naturally.

She stopped, pretending to be exhausted.

"Now what?" he demanded.

Jane exaggerated her breathlessness. "I have to catch my breath." Leaning down, she rested her hands on her knees, like an exhausted runner.

"Look," she said, sounding surprised. She pointed with her bound hands. "Wasn't your sleeping bag a bright blue?"

Montgomery grunted. "We'll go down right here."

Jane didn't think it was the best spot for a descent, but she kept her mouth shut.

"You first," he said.

"Untie my hands." He didn't say anything. "Look how steep this descent is. I need—"

"Get going.

For a moment she studied the terrain. Her best chance to get down without major injuries was to take a zigzag, sideways path. Carefully, she started the descent. She dislodged a small but noisy avalanche of rocks on her way down but didn't fall.

Montgomery copied her maneuver. He, too, got down safely.

"Sorry I didn't break a leg?" he asked with a smirk.

Jane ignored him. If Santiago was anywhere near, he couldn't have missed the racket they'd made or the clear path they'd left behind. That didn't seem to worry Montgomery. Good. Overconfidence was a wonderful flaw.

They walked to last night's camp.

Montgomery motioned her to sit on the ground. She watched him dig through his backpack. He took out a small towel, cut off a long strip, and approached her. Before she realized what he was up to, she felt the material cut painfully into the corners of her mouth. He had effectively gagged her.

She saw him take a big candy bar from his pack and eat it noisily. Jane forced herself not to watch him, to think of something else. What was she going to cook for the rest of the week? In her mind she imagined herself cooking their meals, imagined herself serving them to Santiago, imagined his warm, approving smile.

Montgomery tossed the empty wrapper at her. For a moment she caught the sweet, unmistakable scent of chocolate. She shut out his mean-spirited laughter. She would bake a chocolate cake, dark, rich, with a milk chocolate frosting. Served with strong, fragrant coffee. And a cold glass of milk. Santiago would smile at her. And then they'd kiss and—

Montgomery interrupted her lovely daydream by ripping open a granola bar and munching it. She turned her body toward the rock and away from her tormentor. She maneuvered her hands toward her coat pocket and the gun. She couldn't reach the pocket.

Montgomery walked down the trail a few feet. Jane pulled herself into a kneeling position. She tried again to reach the gun. She couldn't.

Don't give up. Don't you dare give up. Thinking of Marisa, of Santiago, she sat up. She'd try something else.

While walking, she had tested the strength of the kerchief he had used to tie her hands. If she wriggled her hands long enough, she should be able to loosen the knot sufficiently to grab a rock. She could hit him with it if he came close enough.

She could heave it into the bushes to warn Santiago. Anything was better than to wait helplessly for her husband to walk into an ambush.

Her husband. Two of the sweetest words she knew. Words that gave her strength.

She looked at the ground around her. Several good-sized stones lay within reach. She moved them closer, shielding them with her body.

Where was Montgomery? She scooted forward in time to see him take his position behind the trunk of a fallen tree. Anyone coming along the path would be an easy target.

Quickly, her heart beating frantically, she stockpiled an arsenal of stones. Then she looked for the sharpest edge on the rock she leaned against. Lifting her hands, she rubbed the kerchief that bound her hands against it.

The material had been washed many times, weakening it. If she had enough time, Jane was sure she could tear the fabric. Then she'd tear into Montgomery. No way would she let him hurt the man she loved.

Chapter Sixteen

The sun was high in the sky by the time Jane thought she saw the first rip in the kerchief binding her hands. She wiped the sweat out of her eyes—or, rather, the one eye that wasn't swollen shut—and looked again. There was definitely a rip. Encouraged, she twisted the cotton fabric, but that did nothing. With a sigh, she continued to rub the kerchief against the rough surfaces of the rock. The knuckles of her fingers were raw and bleeding, but, gritting her teeth, she continued.

She had dropped her canteen on the path. It was only a few feet away, but it lay where Montgomery might see her retrieve it. Well, so be it. She needed water. Cautiously she crawled to the canteen and dragged it behind the rock. She maneuvered it to her mouth. The water soaked the gag. Finally, a little penetrated into her parched mouth.

Jane wished she had some idea of when Santiago planned to attack. Most likely not until dark. She had to hang tough until then, ignore her growling stomach, ignore her raw, bleeding fingers, ignore the bruises on her body, which hurt devilishly, and concentrate on freeing her hands. Even though Montgomery claimed he wanted to exchange her, she knew he was lying.

She had made good progress when she heard footsteps approach. Quickly, she lowered her hands into her lap and slumped against the rock.

"Hey." Montgomery prodded her with one boot.

Her swollen eye faced him, so she had to turn her whole head to see him. He removed the gag.

"I didn't think I hit you that hard."

"You did."

175

"Eat this. Santiago isn't coming until after dark. Can't have you die on me before then." He tossed a granola bar into her lap.

Food. Her fingers curled around the precious item. Jane restrained herself from ripping the wrapper off the granola bar until she was certain Montgomery was back at his post behind a large rock. The nut-and-fruit bar was delicious. She forced herself to eat slowly, to savor every morsel.

She was about to take a drink of water when she saw Santiago on the path above her. Astonished, she cried out his name before she could stop herself. Unfortunately, her cry was loud enough to alert Montgomery. Shots followed. Jane couldn't tell who'd started the shooting, only that it sounded as if World War III had erupted around her.

The shooting ceased as abruptly as it had started. What was happening? Jane couldn't endure not knowing if Santiago was hit or worse. She stood. Suddenly a strong arm clamped around her chest from behind. Looking at the shirtsleeves, she knew it was Montgomery.

"Hey, El Lobo? I have your woman. You want to talk about a trade?"

"Don't. He'll shoot us anyway!" Jane cried out.

"Shut up," Montgomery muttered, "or I'll cut your throat."

His arm tightened around her until Jane thought he'd crush her chest.

"Hey, El Lobo? What do you say?"

Silence.

Where was Santiago? Dear heaven above, he couldn't be dead. Jane prayed as she had never prayed before. When the silence continued, she knew she had to act. She let herself go completely limp, slumping heavily across Montgomery's left arm.

"What the hell?" he muttered, trying to get a firmer grip on her.

Before he could, Jane drove her right elbow into his abdomen. His grunt and his relaxed hold on her told her the move had been effective. She repeated it, forcing him to let go of her. Before he could raise his weapon, she flung herself at him. He stumbled, staggered back several feet, tottered a moment on the edge of the steep incline, and then toppled over it.

Jane gasped, shocked at what she had done. A hand grabbed her and pulled her back. Santiago.

"Stay back. He may not be dead. I don't want you to be a target." Santiago disappeared in pursuit of Montgomery.

With her hands and feet still bound, Jane dragged herself to the edge. Though she could hear the sound of dislodged stones and earth, she couldn't see either man. She forced herself to breathe deeply. What if Montgomery was the one to come back? Jane couldn't bear the thought. It would be Santiago. It had to be Santiago.

When the trembling of her hands stopped, she tried to shove them into the pocket of her jacket to get the gun. With them still tied, this was apparently impossible. Jane burst into tears.

Stop crying. Pull yourself together.

She hooked the ripped part of the kerchief on one of the sharp edges of the rock and pulled. After what seemed like hours she managed to tear the fabric sufficiently to free her hands. With frantic haste she untied her ankles. Then she pulled the gun from her pocket. With the safety off, she kneeled behind the rock, steadying the gun on top of it, and waited.

The longer she waited, the more anxious she got. What if it wasn't Santiago who came back? What if Montgomery reared his turtle head above the edge? It would mean he'd killed Santiago. Jane repressed a sob. What would she do if the killer returned? What choice did she have? Shoot him or be shot. Could she shoot him?

What would happen to Marisa if Jane were dead too? Who would love her and take care of her? What if that sweet, innocent baby had to pass from foster home to foster home? Or get adopted by some abusive family? Thinking of the beloved child, Jane knew she could shoot Montgomery.

Maybe he wouldn't come back. Wishful thinking.

"Jane? Where are you?"

Santiago's voice. Her knees threatened to collapse. "Over

here." When he swung himself up over the edge, she started to cry and dropped the gun.

Santiago was beside her in a flash. He pulled her into his arms and cradled her.

"It is over, *querida*. Montgomery will never terrorize you again. I am so sorry you had to be drawn into this fight."

When her tears slowed to a mere trickle and she could speak, she said, "I know you said not to leave the ranch, but I thought you were in trouble and—"

"I know. I spoke with Penny."

"Are you okay?" she asked, pulling back in his arms to look at him. "I was so afraid for you. Montgomery is . . . was such a tough, mean man."

"Mean, yes. Tough, no."

"He sounded plenty tough to me."

"*Querida,* those who talk tough generally are not." He lifted her hands. "You freed yourself," he said with admiration. Then, when he saw the cuts and scrapes, the dried blood, his lips thinned. He lifted his canteen to her mouth and let her drink her fill. Then he moistened his kerchief and wiped her face as gently as if she were an infant.

"Your poor face," he said, covering it with gentle kisses. "Your poor mouth." He brushed his lips across hers with infinite care. As he gazed at her face, his voice grew fierce. "I am only sorry that Montgomery went down the ridge before I had a chance to put him through some of the misery he put you through."

"It's okay. It's over." Jane pulled back to look into his eyes, wanting to ask him something.

"What is it, *querida?*"

"How long do you think I'll have to go to jail for killing him?"

Astonished, Santiago stared at Jane. "It was self-defense. He would have killed you without compunction. He tricked you into coming out here, he kidnapped you, and, knowing his warped character, I am sure he tormented you. On top of that, he was a big-time drug lord and killer—"

"But—"

Santiago laid a finger gently across her lips. "Listen to me, *querida*. There isn't a district attorney in the country who would bring charges against you. It was self-defense."

"Still, I threw myself at him and caused him to fall over the edge. I only wanted to stop him so he couldn't shoot you."

"A clear case of self-defense. I am sure Father Anselmo will also tell you that you have the right to defend yourself." Gently he said, "Let's go home. Can you walk back to your truck, or shall I carry you?"

"I can walk," she said, "but it would be nice if you held my hand."

For endless hours after they returned to the ranch, law enforcement officials bombarded them with questions, interviews, statements. Deputy Wilson waited until the DEA agents had finished their questions and driven off with the drugs Santiago had hidden before he approached Jane.

"Hey, Jane. You okay?" Bud asked.

She shrugged.

"From the looks of you and from what the DEA guys told me, you've been through the wringer. Tell me about it."

Jane groaned. "Again?"

"Yeah, for our records. And for possible arrest warrants for some local people who may have been involved in the smuggling ring."

Jane looked at him, realizing that he seemed changed. The bullying facade was gone, replaced by that of a serious and almost compassionate lawman. She told him what had happened. "Bud, I think the sheriff might have known what was going on."

Bud nodded. "He resigned right after the DEA agents arrived, citing poor health. Judging by the way he looked, he really could be sick. He aged ten years today. I don't know what charges, if any, will be brought against him."

"So, you're the acting sheriff?"

"Looks that way. At least until election time." He looked pleased.

"Just don't get greedy," she warned.

"After seeing what the lure of easy money did to the sheriff, you can bet the ranch I won't."

"What about Byron Jones?" she asked.

"The DEA agents picked him up. He cleared Leanne."

"Thank heaven he had the decency to do that. I never doubted that she was innocent. What about Tom Long?"

"He swears all he did was rent them his horses. He had no idea they were running drugs."

"You believe him?" Jane wanted to know.

Bud shrugged. "I don't have any proof, so unless somebody gives him up or I get some evidence, there's nothing I can do."

"You might want to check his finances. Recently he bought a lot of new things, and I know for a fact that cattle prices haven't suddenly skyrocketed."

"I will. You take care."

After Bud left, Father Anselmo arrived.

"Did you bring Marisa?" Jane asked eagerly.

"No. I'll bring her tomorrow. Santiago said you needed rest." Looking at Jane's face, he asked, "Are you sure you don't need a doctor?"

"I'm sure."

"I will feed the horses," Santiago said, "and give you two a chance to talk."

He did the chores, all the time thinking about Jane and what she had been through during the last twenty-four hours. He had not counted on his ex-compadre to involve an innocent woman. That was unlike him. Or it had been. Apparently in his descent into crime and evil he had hit rock bottom. For a moment Santiago felt a stab of regret. Then he hardened his heart. All bets were off. Anyone threatening, much less harming, Jane had crossed all lines. The gloves were off.

When he came back to the house, the padre had left. He found Jane in the kitchen. She was wearing a robe, and, judging by her wet hair, she must have taken a shower.

"How are you feeling?" he asked.

"Better. I can heat some soup and make sandwiches."

"You've been crying."

She nodded.

"Did Father Anselmo say something to upset you?"

"Oh, no. I feel better after talking to him. I think I cried in relief that the nightmare was over."

It wasn't, though, but this was hardly the time to tell her that. He felt a wave of guilt sweep over him. If he could stop this madness, he would, but they had come too far. A final confrontation was inevitable.

"You want some soup?" she asked.

"Soup would be good. I'm going to check the warning systems."

It wasn't until Santiago had left the house that Jane wondered why he had to check the security systems now that Montgomery was dead.

When she woke, bright sunlight flooded the bedroom. For a moment she was disoriented. Then, remembering Santiago putting her to bed, she tried to sit up, only to fall back with a cry of pain.

Santiago rushed to her side. "What is wrong, *querida?*"

"My back," she said.

"Turn over."

She did, slowly, unable to prevent a groan.

Santiago lifted the T-shirt she wore. His breath caught audibly when he saw the bruises. "Did Montgomery do this?"

"No. I lost my footing on the ridge and slid down on my backside."

"Pobrecita." A new wave of guilt assailed Santiago. "I will massage your back, but it will hurt. At least at first."

He stroked her long hair, which spilled in luxurious waves across her back. He didn't think he would ever tire of touching those silken tresses. Gently he caressed her back, which was taut, beautifully muscled. He couldn't stop himself from planting a series of increasingly passionate kisses on her soft skin. Only when Jane moaned softly did he come to his senses. This wasn't the time to caress Jane. She was in pain. Carefully he manipulated her sore muscles.

Jane gritted her teeth against the pain. After a while, though, the sharp edge of the pain dulled, and she felt something akin to pleasure.

"Stay right there while I get the salve," he said.

"The one that smells like turpentine and marigolds?"

He chuckled. "But it is effective."

When he returned, he applied the salve with tender fingers. "You know what? I like the smell of turpentine and marigolds on you," he murmured. "Stay like that to give the salve a chance to work." And give him a chance to get ready.

When Jane awoke the second time, she felt better. After soaking in an almost scalding hot bathtub for fifteen minutes, she was able to get dressed and tend to the horses.

Outside, a pleasant breeze ruffled her hair. As she crossed the yard, movement caught her eye—movement from the flagpole. She frowned. She hadn't flown a flag since Memorial Day. Shading her eyes against the sun, she looked up at the pole. A piece of red fabric fluttered in the wind. It was Santiago's old red T-shirt. What on earth was it doing up there?

Before she could pursue that puzzle, the warning system went off. Jane turned toward the house, ready to take defensive measures, when she remembered that that was no longer necessary.

She stopped in the yard and waited. A couple of minutes later a pickup truck stopped near her. Penny rushed toward Jane.

"Are you okay?" she asked. "All kinds of stories are floating around about smuggling and kidnapping and stuff like that."

"For once the stories are true."

"Mercy! Tell me everything," Penny said, her voice eager.

"It all started with the phone call you got, the one from Santiago. . . ." Jane's voice trailed off as the truth dawned on her. How could she have been so dense?

"What? Go on."

"Why? You know what happened—knew before it happened."

"What are you talking about? How could I know?"

"You're part of it. Up to now I thought only Tom was involved, but you're knee-deep in the smuggling as well."

"I don't know where you'd get that crazy idea from, but—"

"Save your breath, Penny. The phone call. Santiago never called you. It was Montgomery."

"No, no. Don't you think I know Santiago's voice?"

"Exactly. His voice and slight accent are distinctive. Remember, you told me once that his voice was sexy? Montgomery could not have imitated the way Santiago talks."

"You're all wrong," Penny said, backing toward the pickup.

"You've been in cahoots with Montgomery all along. I wondered how he knew I'd be at the clinic. You told him."

"You have no proof."

"No, I don't, but the IRS will find it once they look at your financial records. They're very good at that sort of thing. Why, Penny? We've been neighbors for years. Friends, even. You almost got me killed. Why? You sold me out for new kitchen appliances?"

"I don't know what you're talking about," Penny repeated.

She jumped into the truck and drove off, splattering gravel in all directions.

Jane sighed. Even if the IRS couldn't prove Penny's involvement, she had lost a friend and a neighbor.

Her gaze strayed to the flagpole. Santiago must have hoisted the piece of fabric. There was no one else. A signal. It had to be a signal. If a white flag meant peace, a red flag denoted what? A red flag waved in front of a bull? A challenge. Santiago had issued a challenge. Her stomach felt as if she'd swallowed a quart of acid.

Santiago's fight with the smugglers wasn't over. Who was left? *The head honcho.* The earth swayed. She rushed to the porch. She clutched the railing, willing herself not to throw up, not to pass out.

She heard Santiago approach but didn't raise her head.

"What is wrong?" he asked.

"What are you planning to do?" she asked.

"Work around the place." He looked around as if assessing the buildings. "Father Anselmo called. He wants you to come and pick up Marisa."

Jane straightened up. "Liar," she whispered. "You're meeting the head honcho, and you want me out of the way."

Santiago heaved a sigh. "Yes," he said after a lengthy silence. "I *would* feel much better if you were safely in town. I am sorry I tried to deceive you, but I didn't think you would go if I asked you."

"Darn straight I wouldn't leave this ranch."

"Not even if I begged you to leave?" he asked softly.

"If I begged you to stay, would you?" She watched him. "I didn't think so."

"I have no choice," he said.

"Yes, you do. No one is forcing you to go."

"Only the voices of the dead."

Jane opened and closed her mouth. What could she say to that? Santiago went inside. She followed him. Watching him take the M-16, the handgun, and the wicked-looking knife energized her. She had to stop him.

"Don't the voices of the living count? Don't Marisa's and my voice count?" she demanded.

"Of course they count. More than you can imagine."

"Then don't go."

"*Querida,* I have to. I swore on my sister's grave that justice would be done."

"Are you sure it's not vengeance you're looking for?"

He framed her face with his hands and kissed her. "I promise I will come back."

"How can you be sure of that? You can't! Don't go. I love you."

Santiago kissed her again with heartbreaking tenderness. Then he turned toward the door.

"I said I loved you. That means nothing to you?"

"It means more than you can know."

"But you're still going?"

"I have to. I will be home before dark."

Jane watched him close the door behind him before sobs tore from her burning throat. Though tears almost blinded her, she took the shotgun from the closet and ran after him.

"I'm going with you as soon as I saddle my horse."

"No. I have to meet him alone."

"Man to man? That's such horse manure!"

"You don't mean that. I know you believe in honor and principles," he said.

"Not when they endanger you."

"Jane, you can't come. If you attempt to follow, I'll call it off, and then I'll lose the advantage of place and time. You have to stay here."

She threw up her hands in despair.

Santiago mounted his horse.

He was leaving. She was losing him, and there was nothing she could do. "Please don't go," she begged once more. She wasn't sure he heard her. Even if he did, he didn't stop.

Chapter Seventeen

Jane slumped on the top porch step, feeling defeated, angry, desperate, and sick to her soul. Kiley came and sat beside her. As if sensing her distress, the dog laid her head in Jane's lap.

How long she'd sat there, she didn't know. The first thing she became aware of was Father Anselmo's car coming to a stop in the yard. Kiley ran to meet him.

The padre sat beside Jane and placed a comforting arm around her shoulders, causing her to burst into tears again.

"You couldn't stop him from going either?" he asked.

She shook her head. "You tried to stop him?"

"Yes."

"He's going to get himself killed. Or he'll kill that man and spend the rest of his life in prison. In either case, I'll lose him." More tears trickled down her face. "And what about Marisa? He's the only blood relative she's got left. Didn't he think about her?"

"He did. He asked me to help you raise her in case he didn't come back."

That statement caused another burst of tears.

"Jane, if you don't stop crying, your other eye will swell shut."

"I know it's dumb to cry. I never cry. I haven't cried in years, and now I can't stop. What's wrong with me?"

"You're hurting."

Jane accepted the handkerchief the padre offered her and dried her eyes. She heaved a big sigh. "I'm done crying."

"Maybe we should make coffee. I'm sure Santiago could use some when he gets back," he suggested.

"*If* he gets back. You know what makes me so angry?"

"What?"

"That it's okay for men to ride out and face danger but not for women. We're supposed to sit at home and wait passively while our fate is being decided. It's so unfair."

"It is, but I can also understand Santiago's point of view. He needs to concentrate on what he's doing without having to worry about your safety."

"Well, that's too bad, because I'm through being passive."

She picked up her shotgun and headed for the barn.

"Jane, look." Father Anselmo pointed to the west.

Jane looked. "Father, tell me that those two riders aren't a mirage."

"They're real. What horse did Santiago take?"

"Red Rover. That's the horse the first man is riding. The question is, is he leading the second horse, or is the man on it holding a gun on Santiago?"

Jane ran into the house and got the binoculars. Her hands shook so badly, Father Anselmo had to take the binoculars.

"It's Santiago, and he's leading the second horse. The man on it is handcuffed."

Jane closed her eyes. She swayed. Father Anselmo placed a calming arm around her shoulders. They stood side by side until Santiago dismounted and tied both horses to the hitching post.

Jane threw herself into Santiago's arms. He held her close for a moment. "Padre, do you mind keeping an eye on this man? I have to phone Deputy Wilson."

"I don't mind."

With an arm around her shoulders, Santiago led Jane into the house. He kicked the door shut with one foot. He spent the next minutes kissing Jane, his love for her dancing like flames in his blood.

"Don't you have to call Bud?" Jane asked, her voice soft.

"I already did. I wanted an excuse to come inside so I could kiss you."

"I was so afraid for you—"

"I know. I am sorry I put you through this, but you must

understand that for months and months only the thought of killing that man out there kept me going."

"But you didn't kill him. Thank heaven you didn't."

"I thought about what you said. What Father Anselmo said. And I couldn't do it."

"What did the padre say?"

"That revenge would poison my life and by extension yours and Marisa's. I couldn't do that to you."

"I'm so relieved," she murmured.

"You said something else. Something more important: that you loved me."

"Yes."

"If I killed him, I might also kill your love. I couldn't risk that. You see, I realized that I loved you too. And love is infinitely more important than revenge."

Jane's throat closed. She fought more tears, but these were tears of happiness. She nodded. "Much more important."

"I also realized that my sister wouldn't hold me to my promise. She would choose love over revenge and retribution."

"Yes, she would. Most women would."

"Thank heaven for women. Thank heaven for you." Santiago kissed her until the blast of a car horn announced the arrival of the deputy sheriff.

"I suppose we'd better go and get rid of the last bad, dark remnant of my old life."

"You mean that? Is ranching going to be enough after the adrenaline-packed life you've led? Ranching and maybe writing on long winter evenings?"

"Yes. You don't know how I've longed for a family, for a home, for love." Santiago kissed her again and again until a discreet knocking on the door brought them back to reality.

"We have to ask Father Anselmo to do something for us," Santiago said.

"What?"

"Marry us in church. Would you like that? Would he?"

"We'd both like it," Jane said, her eyes shining with love.